There's a Monster in the Woods

BOOK 0.5

Spooky BOYS

FAE QUIN

There's a Monster in the Woods

SPOOKY BOYS 0.5

Cover Art and Interior Artwork by Fae Loves Art

WWW.FAELOVESART.COM

Typography and Interior Formatting by We Got You Covered Book Design

WWW.WEGOTYOUCOVEREDBOOKDESIGN.COM

Dedicated to my husband

without whom my dreams would've remained dreams.

For anyone who's ever wanted

to bang the monster in the fairytale.

Author Note

HELLO EVERYONE! Thank you so much for picking up this copy of *There's a Monster in the Woods*. This book is near and dear to me as it is technically the first book I ever shared with you! Though, this rendition has received a rewrite as well as new interior art, never before seen scenes, and a new cover—it is still just as precious to me as the original version. Maybe even more so now that I've gotten a chance to share these babies with you a second time.

Styx and Ellis are such a special couple. With their playfulness, their softness, and their devotion from day one, I loved getting to dive back into their fairytale. I hope you enjoy reading the newly revamped version as much as I enjoyed writing it!

While this book has a lot of humor throughout, it deals with some dark elements. A full content list is up on my website and my Instagram for anyone that would like to know what they're diving into before they begin. I can't wait to hear what you all think! As always, feel free to reach out to me while you're reading, and all reviews, comments, and shares are greatly appreciated. I love you all so much, enjoy!

WWW.FAELOVESART.COM

There's a monster in the woods.
That's what the stories always say.
With gnashing teeth,
And wind for wings,
Little children are its prey.

There's a monster in the woods.
At night you'll hear its mournful cries.
And off the path,
You'll feel its wrath,
Be wary of yellow eyes.

There's a monster in the woods.
And if you listen close,
You'll hear its cry,
Echo through the sky,
Its call for blood inside its throat.

Chapter One

BEING THE TOWN outcast had its perks. No one invited me out anymore. No one expected me to participate in town functions, parties, or parades. And, aside from polite chit chat, no one delved into the complexities of my life. I'm sure most people would find it boring anyway.

Which was exactly how I liked it.

Boring.

No matter what the townspeople murmured behind closed doors, and down the cobblestone streets, nothing ever bothered me. Maybe it had once upon a time, when I hadn't fully embraced my lifestyle yet. But now? Nearly thirty with what felt like a lifetime of practice? Yeah, I honestly couldn't care less.

I'd heard it all.

The whispers, the judgment, the pitying looks hidden behind hats and hands, eyes and lips that spoke quietly in the hopes I wouldn't hear.

Ellis hasn't left his house in weeks, they'd whisper.

Twenty-seven years old with no future in sight.

That boy will rot alone with only his dog and his vegetables for company.

He's too quiet, too… blah, blah, blah.

They probably weren't meant to make me laugh, but I'd never understood social cues. Truthfully, I cared about the rumors as much as I cared about the next episode of whatcha-ma-call-it I overheard everyone raving about when I came into town. Which was to say, not at all.

I didn't care what they thought of me.

That's what I told myself anyway.

Because the moment I started to care I'd surely break, and I refused to ever get to that point.

I scuffed my already dirty sneakers on the linoleum as I waited patiently in line for my turn at the cash register. It was surprisingly busy at the shop today. The chatter of the patrons behind me made my skin crawl and my hands tremble. It set my teeth on edge too, in the way only going into town ever managed to do.

The basket in my grip rattled as I steadied myself with a calming breath, hovering protectively over its contents. I'd gathered a large variety of vegetable seeds this year, though I hadn't bought any pumpkin seeds for the fall despite spending hours preparing a space in my garden specifically for them. I'd already decided it was a year for plentiful fruits and vegetables, not for dealing with Farmer Jones's wrath.

At this rate I'd never plant them, but I was content to focus on my other endeavors to avoid unnecessary conflict.

I'd always liked gardening.

It calmed me.

I spent my childhood wearing oversized, patched-up overalls. From spring to fall I had soil beneath my fingernails and pollen inside my nose.

The moment the sun was up, so was I, soaking up its rays, covered head to toe in dirt as I learned how to love the earth properly, guided by my Aunt June and Uncle Ruth's forever patient hands.

Vegetables had rules if you wanted them to thrive.

Spring was the time to plant the hardiest of cool season crops: broccoli, asparagus, onion, and peas. After the last frost came time for the half-hardy ones: Celery, lettuce, and potatoes. And then, when the last of the chill had left the air, it came time for the tender vegetables: Cucumbers, peppers, tomatoes, and squash.

I didn't have the courage to plant pumpkins this year, but I figured there would be plenty of time for me to build it up before next spring. Maybe. If I ever did. There were dozens of other plants to worry about until then.

I was feeling rather perky about the whole thing as I plopped my basket onto the counter and gave the clerk what I hoped was a sufficiently friendly nod. He was shorter than me—most people I met were—and I ducked my head, avoiding his gaze. Shoving my trembling hands in my pockets hid them from prying eyes, and I relaxed a fraction until I realized my mistake. With my eyes darting around I'd accidentally caught a glimpse of my own unwelcome reflection in the window behind him.

Ugh.

I was a tall, gangly, brown-haired blur, dressed in stained overalls, my sun hat perched like a shield atop my head—

"Ellis," he grunted, just as he always did.

"Hiya, Tom." I smiled at him, tapping my feet a little as I painstakingly waited for him to ring up each of my items. They rattled on their way back into my basket and with each one that fell safely inside, I relaxed.

"Planting season again I see."

"Every spring." My smile was harder to maintain the longer I felt his eyes on my face, his movements somehow growing even more unhurried. Jesus Christ, could the man be any *slower*? My smile continued to wobble, though I miraculously maintained it, hoping the friendliness would encourage him to work faster.

It did not.

"Good luck." Tom hummed after I paid, pushing the basket my way again.

I always brought my own basket. It was easier than trying to juggle plastic bags all the way home. The benefit to the environment was another motivating factor. I'd do anything to avoid the crinkling sound the plastic made. It always set my teeth on edge and made my head spin.

Ellis hates plastic bags, what a travesty! Blah, blah, blah.

I could practically hear the rumors already.

I knew I was strange, but I'd never felt the need to change. I always just figured it wasn't my fault I hadn't been properly socialized as a child. I'd grown up loved, just the way I was, and I interacted so infrequently with the outside world I didn't feel the need to change just to make them more comfortable.

We'd lived in our own little world, just my Aunt and Uncle and me. The sun and moon dictated our schedule. I'd only really left the little bubble they created after they died and I realized I'd need to learn to go into town for the things I couldn't grow or make myself.

People were… hard.

Talking to them was harder.

It wasn't that I didn't like them—because I did. Truly. They were fascinating, with their colorful clothing, their hair dye, and their naturally suspicious nature. Like brightly feathered birds strutting around with their necks bobbing and cell phones to their ears. They almost acted as though the second they ceased attachment to technology they'd simply stop existing.

It was as hilarious as it was foreign.

I'd never understood *that* either.

Cellphones, I mean.

I had a single landline my entire childhood and I never intended to change that, despite the fact that the phone was more than likely older than I was. I abhorred every time it rang. I couldn't imagine voluntarily having a device on my body that opened up the option for constant communication. I'd probably die.

My house was on the north end of town. It lay at the end of a winding dirt road, hidden between cornfields and the occasional farmhouse, as far away from civilization as my Aunt and Uncle had been able to manage. Most everything—all the businesses, the schools, the residential areas, and the fairgrounds—were located south of the woods. The trees acted as a protective barrier. I couldn't blame my family for coveting their peaceful solitude. I understood the need for quiet more than most. The burning desire to escape from the world and its constant noise.

Maybe sometimes it was lonely, when the nights grew too quiet, and even the steady *thump, thump* of Rotho's tail against the floorboards couldn't chase away the weight of the silence—but still, I would rather *that* than deal with the overstimulation of being surrounded by people day in and day out. *No thank you.*

Despite what the gossipers had theorized it meant about me as a person, it had never bothered me that our humble little cottage and massive, frankly *wonderful* garden were located smack dab against the border of the forest.

I'd never taken much stock in rumors, and even though I was alone now I appreciated the whisper of the trees and didn't mind the so-called danger they posed.

There were two ways home.

The long way and the short way.

The long way wound around the woods, never crossing beneath the branches of the trees, always far enough away from the greedy boughs even the shadows couldn't touch you.

It was the safe way.

The socially acceptable choice.

I never took it.

I always opted for the other shorter option. The one that led directly into the forest and cut off a good forty-five minutes of walking time. It was more efficient that way, and I'd never been frightened by the stories like the other children had. Plus, I liked the way the scent of the woods clung to my skin for days after walking through it. I liked listening to the birds cry as they flitted between branches. I liked the way the wind whistled through the air, caressing my hair almost like a long-lost friend.

Maybe I *should've* been afraid. Even though I'd grown up under a rock, I was still very aware of the stories that surrounded our forest. Uttered like the words were cursed themselves, the myths painted in ignorance and fear.

The woods are haunted, some people said.

A demon inhabits them, others countered.

But most common of all was the theory that the children's poem we'd all chanted as kids was true after all. We'd grown hoarse from the force of our singing as the tale of caution vibrated innocently through the air, an invisible companion as we flitted from playground to playground, and down the leaf strewn streets.

There's a monster in the woods, the poem clearly states.

I had my doubts.

In all my years cutting through the forest, I had never seen a monster. I was skeptical it had ever existed at all, despite the yearly town 'Sacrifice.' I wasn't alone in that skepticism. The tradition was outdated and unnecessary considering the fact that it had been hundreds of years since the 'monster' had taken any of the Sacrifices it was given. Even still though, the townspeople avoided the woods like the plague.

I was always alone inside them, just the way I liked it.

The forest was surprisingly chilly that day, the familiar caress of the wind against my skin soothing despite the way I shivered. The howl of the breeze flitting through open branches followed me as I walked over the sun-dappled overgrown path.

It was a good day.

Despite the fact I'd gone into town.

I much preferred the solitude of home and the company of my dog. Rotho was my toothy best friend. Snow white with big tawny brown splotches dotted throughout his thick fur. I adopted him when he was just a puppy. He'd been a tiny thing. Fragile. Sweet. He'd stared up at me with these huge soulful brown eyes, his head tilted to the side like he wasn't sure if he could trust me. I'd fallen in love right then.

I had a thing for strays; I always had. Most of the time I felt like a stray myself.

That natural distrust was what had drawn me to him in the first place.

Rotho's kennel at the local pound had declared him an Australian Shepherd, though as he'd grown, I figured he must've been a mix. His legs were just slightly too long, his snout a bit too stubby. His nose was beginning to speckle with gray now, but those big brown eyes remained the same. He was as perfect now as he'd been then, though admittedly he judged me more often now than he had when I'd been a kid. Oftentimes Rotho was the only being I talked to for weeks on end, which was exactly as I preferred it.

I missed him now, as I walked along in silence, dry dirt crunching beneath the soles of my boots.

The canopy above was tall enough I couldn't help but compare it to the buildings I'd seen illustrated on magazines and posters throughout the town square. *Huh. What would that feel like?* To tip your head back and see metal and brick climb high enough it blocked out the sun. To be surrounded by man-made things, the scent of plastic, of steel—No. *No.* I didn't like that at all. My pulse skyrocketed as I forced the thoughts away.

Maybe the city was majestic to some, but just thinking about it made me feel claustrophobic.

Trees were far less intimidating than skyscrapers. They were alive in a way the city never could be. *You could feel them breathe.* I shuddered out a relieved sigh as I focused on the present to slow the stutter of my heart. I couldn't help but smile as the sun trickled between branches and caught on the calloused pads of my tanned fingertips. I turned my hands over to admire the play of sunlight, stopping for just a moment, my grip on my basket loose.

I was nearly to the edge of the forest when I heard an unfamiliar noise. I'd spent so much time in the woods, you'd think that would be impossible. Curious, I cocked my head to the side, scanning the tree line. Tree branches creaked as I blew a lock of hair out of my eyes, holding perfectly still while I listened.

There. To the left.

A sharp, broken sort of cry.

Maybe an animal of some kind? I wasn't sure. I didn't like feeling that way. Unsettled.

My basket slipped from the nervous sweat on my palms. I adjusted my grip, knuckles white as I whipped around to face the sound. There was nothing lurking between the tree trunks, and my heart lurched as I forced back my panic. Nothing appeared out of the ordinary. Just leaves and brambles, bark and crickets.

Maybe I'd imagined it?

Breathing through my growing panic, I forced myself to move a few wobbly steps down the path. This was fine. Everything was fine. Of course it was. I'd just scared myself, remembering the children's tale. That's all this was. *Paranoia.* I froze as the almost pained howl echoed a third and final time before the forest settled, silent once again.

I hadn't imagined it.

It was clear to me now the noise was coming from off the path, past a thick copse of trees that looked like it might hide a clearing. I could hear running water, spring bright in the air, as I made the split-second decision to help.

The animal could be hurt.

I couldn't leave it there.

I just couldn't.

Monster be damned.

My basket remained clutched tight in my slick grip, the seeds rattling as I pushed off the path and into the bushes for the first time. Despite using this shortcut for most of my life, I'd never dared to step off the path and into the woods themselves.

The part of me that was practical knew suspecting the monster might be real was silly. But then again, my town had a yearly Sacrifice, so I felt my paranoia was at least a bit precedented.

I clearly remembered holding onto my aunt's fingers as she laughed and pointed up at the platform the Sacrifice had been tied to. Blue ribbons twined around naked limbs, twisting like vines, as the sun set and the crowds parted, the scent of cornbread and apple cider donuts drifting through the air. The juxtaposition between the festivities and the captured figure atop the platform had lurked in the back of my mind from the moment I'd seen it, no matter how many years went by. When we'd gone home after dark and the fair had ended, year after year, the Sacrifice remained.

Never stolen, the way the stories predicted.

The first time I'd seen a Sacrifice, I'd thought he'd been covered in blood. I'd stared, and stared, *and stared*—Aunt June had snorted and shook her head when she'd seen the look on my face. She'd taken me by the cheeks, her grip gentle, eyes twinkling, as she proudly proclaimed that *that* was the entire point of the paint in the first place. In fact, the first Sacrifices several hundred years ago *had* been covered in pig's blood to entice the monster out of the woods. It would take them away, feast upon them, and the town would remain safe from its hunger for another year.

It was a twisted fairytale but a fairytale nonetheless.

There was no reason for me to be frightened now, I rationalized as my heart pounded and I crept my way deeper into the woods.

No one truly believed the monster existed anymore, and the Sacrifice had become an honor with no price tag attached. In fact, instead of death, you received prestige along with a hefty reward if selected. The whole thing was still macabre though. Despite seeing the red-splashed people every fall for as long as I could remember, the sight never got any less jarring.

Maybe that was why I felt so unnerved.

Yes.

That was it.

Not because I'd just done the exact thing I'd been warned not to do my entire life.

The trees almost seemed to part for me as I stepped deeper and deeper into their shadows. It was a strange sort of sensation. I fit in more here between tree trunks than I ever had sandwiched between bodies. The trees were friendlier, kinder, quieter. Their long branches swayed as I traipsed underneath them. The way they waved in the flickering wind felt—

Welcoming.

Foreboding.

Hopeful?

I could see the clearing I'd predicted would be there through gaps in the trees, and when I finally reached the edge of it, I paused behind a massive gnarled oak tree. My heart rattled around in my chest as I stepped in close to stay out of sight. I set my basket down, as quietly as I could. It rattled a bit, but the sound was lost between the chirps of the birds overhead.

Cool bark scratched against my palms and I held my breath, listening for signs of the creature I'd heard. I knew hiding was silly, but I did it anyway. *Hadn't I come out here to help?* Hiding was not helping. What if there really was an injured animal out there? What if it needed me? I couldn't do anything if I didn't look. My heart stuttered as I took a steadying breath and peeked.

At first, I didn't see anything.

The sun was too bright where it shone on the tall grass, its light golden.

It took my eyes a moment to adjust, and when they did, I bit my lip hard to hold back the cry that threatened to escape.

I'd been wrong all along.

Because in the center of the clearing was no common forest animal. It was a creature unlike anything I'd ever seen before.

Its body was large and slightly too lean for its height. It had skin tanned from the sun, much like my own, though its limbs faded into a blackened flesh that looked leathery and almost charred. Long black claws severed the flesh of the deer the beast had pinned beneath it. Atop its head sat a pair of gorgeous black antlers that glinted in the sunlight as its broad shoulders flexed. Every movement it made was with purpose, a killing machine crowned with a swath of earthy dark curls that obscured what looked to be an entirely human face.

Huh.

It moved, rising slowly, steadily, muscles rippling as it stood on two feet, blood splattered across its pecs and sculpted abs. Shocked by the sight, I remained frozen, unable to do anything but stare.

The creature was… a *man*.

That much was made clear the moment I caught sight of the full glory of his naked body. A thick cock lay nestled inside a riot of dark curls that matched the ones on his head. *Hot.* Suddenly I was hot all over, my cheeks burned, and my mouth grew suspiciously dry. His dick twitched, swinging a little as he took a careful step around his prey, his thick thighs flexing. I forced my gaze up, cheeks burning, confusion buzzing like bees beneath my skin, a companion to my fear.

Everything had happened so quickly. Those few seconds felt like lifetimes.

The cloying metallic scent of blood hit me like a sledgehammer. Copper burned inside my nose, sickness welling like acid inside me as I watched long claws slide slick and wet through deer flesh while the creature crouched over his prey once again. He feasted hungrily, little grunts and growls echoing through the air as he ate his fill. His antlers reached toward the treetops, and I noticed with a revolted lurch that splatters of blood had decorated the black bone.

I suppose in a way it was as beautiful a sight as it was terrifying.

Nature at its finest, predator and prey.

There was no helping the deer now, so my thoughts naturally turned to the other obvious prey in the clearing. *Me.*

My heart was in my throat, beating erratically, rabbit-like and terrified. Each breath felt like a foghorn in the silence.

Would the creature want to hunt me if I ran?

Could he smell my fear?

My excitement?

How was this even real?

I'd heard all the stories as a child and I'd always thought the monster was a myth, but… there was nothing made up about the creature in front of me. He was as real as I was, flesh and blood.

I took a careful step backward, hoping to ease my way toward the path without being noticed. The first few steps I managed without incident and then—

Crack.

The noise of the branch I stepped on was loud enough it echoed. A bird took flight in the distance, the flap of its wings thrumming like the ticking arms of a clock as icy dread filled my veins.

I watched—almost in slow motion—as the creature raised his head for the second time that day. His bangs swooped far enough to the side that I caught a glimpse of his gleaming yellow eyes, just as the poem had always warned. Almost cat-like. A panther waiting to pounce.

And off the path

You'll feel its wrath

Be wary of yellow eyes.

With his eyes staring into mine like that, there was no way I could deny that he was striking in a wild sort of way. There was dirt smudged across the bridge of his nose, and his ears were hidden by chaotic curls so dark they were nearly black. Like soil right after a rainstorm. Everything about his face was human, inviting, masculine. His nose was hooked in a way that made something dangerous flip in the pit of my stomach as I watched his tongue flick out—bright red—before retreating back inside his mouth. His eyes were curious and as I stared, panic burst white-hot in my chest.

Terrified of the creature and the feelings looking at him incited, I did the only thing I could.

I ran.

Branches whipped my skin, the wind pulling like fingers at my back, almost like it didn't want me to leave. Every new cut ached as my blood pounded frantically. My breath shuddered as it squeezed its way through my overworked lungs, and my leg muscles burned as I dodged between tree trunks, working back the way I'd come as quickly as I could.

And then, *finally*, there was freedom.

My feet hit the path again, and I continued all the way home, listening for the sound of footsteps behind me.

I didn't realize until after I'd showered off the fear and settled into bed for the night with Rotho laying his heavy, furry body like a blanket across my chest, that I'd left my basket in the woods, seeds abandoned for nature to take hold of them.

I'd have to go into town again. Just thinking about it made me cringe. Rotho's familiar sleepy-doggy snores filled my head and my heart, and after what felt like a century I was finally able to relax.

This time I'd take the long way.

Everything would be fine.

It wasn't like the monster had followed me home, right? It couldn't leave the woods. It certainly never had before, otherwise I would've heard about it by now. Rotho snuffled and I buried my head in his curls, lulled into sleep as I forced myself to forget about my nightmare of an afternoon.

Through the crack in the window, the wind whistled. My hanging plants swayed, and my eyelids drooped as I listened close. *Had the wind always sounded like that?* Like the mournful cries from the fairytale that didn't feel real from inside the safety of my little cottage? I fell asleep to the song of sadness, my eyes too heavy to keep open, despite the echo of loneliness threatening to cave in my chest.

There's a monster in the woods.

And if you listen close,

You'll hear its cry,

Echo through the sky,

Its call for blood inside its throat.

Chapter Two

I MUST'VE IMAGINED dropping the basket.

There was no other way to explain the fact that I'd woken up that morning, gone out to my garden to enjoy my morning cup of tea, and found the basket sitting in the dirt right where I planned to plant my tomatoes.

Maybe I'd dropped it on my way into the house?

I scratched my head, confused.

Rotho bounded ahead of me, his long tail swishing as he sniffed around the basket and dug his cold nose between the seed packets. They rattled under his attention, and I laughed, shaking my head in amusement. After sniffing it for a solid minute, Rotho decided it was safe and scurried off to investigate the rustling of a squirrel out in the open field between our cottage and the tree line.

Being this close to the woods had never made me uneasy before. With my basket in front of me, however, I was forced to come to the conclusion that I must've imagined my day in the woods. Physical evidence, after all, pointed in that direction. *Maybe I was overworked?*

I frowned and made my way over to the basket, inspecting it myself. It looked normal enough. No scratches. Maybe it was a bit dirty, but otherwise it looked untouched. Relaxing, I sat in the dirt to take inventory of the seed packets while I sipped at my lukewarm Earl Grey.

The mellow, almost citrusy flavor tickled my taste buds as it always did, and I sighed into the warmth of it, rifling through the basket. I systematically laid out the ones I'd need to plant that day if I wanted them to grow before the end of summer. I knew their planting order by heart.

The forest loomed in my peripheral vision, but I did my best to ignore it and the fact that it lay only a hundred or so yards from my home. I'd always liked having it close, but now I wasn't sure how to feel. The land at the edge of the forest had always been cheaper than the land closer to the highway. My Aunt had loved to listen to the woods rustle at night, and we'd often sat outside in the dirt as the nighttime creatures began to wake. She'd liked the privacy. I always had too.

Now I couldn't help but wonder if too much privacy was a bad thing. No one could hear you scream.

But no.

No.

There was no monster.

If there had been, I wouldn't be holding my basket like I was. Monsters did not pick up baskets and return them. That was more absurd than imagining a monster in the woods in the first place. Therefore I had to have made up the whole thing.

That was the *only* logical explanation.

I'd been known to have a rather vivid imagination.

Mystery solved, I shrugged away my unease and headed inside to wash my now empty cup. Feeling rejuvenated, I returned a few minutes later in my usual gardening gear—a pair of loose overalls, a large sun hat, and sunglasses that were more functional than stylish. The wind echoed, but I ignored it. I had plans. Pushing aside thoughts of monsters, and cocks, and the way they made me feel, I pulled my gloves on, knelt in the cool dirt, and got to work.

Weeks passed, and everything seemed normal. I headed into town several times to stock up on perishables, ignoring the looks everyone gave me as I wandered around in a daze, dirt-stained and sunburnt. The first couple of trips I took the long way home, avoiding the monster I wasn't even sure existed.

My vivid imagination had started to feel like a curse.

Because sometimes—it might've been a trick of the light—it seemed like there was a shadow following politely behind me. Fifteen paces or so back, a figure in the woods that flickered between tree trunks as I made my way home with my arms full and my head even fuller.

By the end of July, I was certain I'd imagined the whole thing. And for the first time since March, I decided to take the shortcut through the woods.

I was tired, and it was too hot to be outside much longer, especially considering how long I'd spent working in my garden that morning. Rotho had been enjoying his time in the sun too, and he'd accompanied me into town today despite the fact I rarely took him.

He was incredibly well-behaved, but I didn't like the way people looked at me when I had him with me. Like they thought I couldn't take care of him because I was quiet. *Different.* Because I didn't know what a 'Tweet' was, and the only time I'd ever used Google was at the local library when I'd been in school.

I could guess what it was, sure. I wasn't *actually* a hermit. But that didn't mean I wanted any part of it. The only tweets I cared about were the ones birds made. I was content to spend my days like I always had, soaking up sunshine with my hands in the dirt and Rotho's slobber on my arms. He had a tendency to lick me whenever I got sweaty. It was as gross as it was endearing.

As always, the heat got more bearable the moment I stepped inside the woods. Branches stretched toward the sun and I sighed, rubbing a hand across my forehead to wipe off the summer sweat as I glanced down at Rotho's happy face, his tongue lolling, brown eyes full of exhaustion and excitement.

It hadn't been this hot when we'd set out that morning, but it was midday now, and I was sincerely regretting my choice to take him.

"Sorry buddy," I said, shifting my basket onto one arm so I could reach down to pet him. We'd run out of water before even hitting the forest.

My throat was parched, my lips painfully dry, as I picked up my pace along the overgrown path in the hopes of getting us home sooner. I knew there was a creek in the woods. I'd heard it that day that I'd imagined the monster, though I hadn't seen it then.

Hopefully I hadn't imagined it too.

When we neared where I'd veered off the path last time, Rotho sat on his fat fluffy ass and refused to move. I was panting too, so I didn't blame him as I sighed and shoved the brim of my hat up again so I could see better.

We had another ten minutes at least before we got home if I took into account all the stops he'd need to take to catch his breath…

Rotho continued to pant beside me. He looked so pitiful like that. Adorable too. His big eyes were beseeching.

I could probably find the creek.

All I'd have to do was listen.

I sighed, staring into his tired brown eyes, a droplet of sweat trickling down the side of my neck. *Fine.* There was no other choice really. I slapped at the sweat droplets absentmindedly as I made my decision.

I'd either have to carry him all the way home or we'd have to stop for water.

Water was the obvious choice.

With my mind made up, I set my basket full of food on the ground at my feet and crouched to look him in the eye. "You're a sweet boy but you sure are trouble sometimes," I told him, scratching along his furry white cheeks as he blinked at me, his tongue flopping out of the side of his mouth. "Alright," I sighed, patting him on the head before I turned towards the forest and closed my eyes to listen.

Branches creaked, a squirrel scuttled, and two tiny birds cooed at each other overhead. Ah. There it was.

That same twinkling sound whispered through the other noises, calling to me.

This time, stepping off the path was a more frightening experience. I had my imagination to thank for that. But I forced myself to push through the unease as I stroked along Rotho's thick, dusty fur and we made our way toward the sound of tinkling water.

I wasn't worried about my basket being stolen. In all my life, I'd never seen another person enter the woods, so I'd felt safe leaving it along the path to pick up after our little detour. It was easy enough finding the stream, and Rotho drank greedily as I filled our water bottle, my body on high alert.

Every rustle in the brush, every snap of twigs, every flap of wings caused anxiety to tighten my throat again. My heart rattled away. Nervously, I scanned our surroundings for threats. Speckled patches of daylight decorated the ground around us, splashing sunshine onto Rotho's white and brown coat like he was a watercolor painting come to life.

After a few minutes on high alert, I finally relaxed. If a monster had been nearby I'd surely have been his lunch by now, wouldn't I? Therefore there was none, and I was being paranoid.

The creek was beautiful.

Calm.

Serene.

How many years had I wasted staying on the same, boring path, when this was just a few steps away? With a sigh I plopped onto a boulder and kicked off my boots to dip my aching feet into the cool water. Rotho splashed around for a bit, and I snorted a laugh as he got my overalls wet with his enthusiasm. Anxiety bled away as I sunk my shins into the icy creek depths and enjoyed the play of light across the tops of my feet underwater.

I was pruny and grinning by the time we'd had our fill.

Rotho lapped at stray droplets on my calves as I dried my feet in a patch of sunlight, before I forced my boots back on over slightly damp socks. There was a rustle in the trees behind me and I whipped around, terrified all over again, only to realize we were still completely alone.

Right.

Paranoid.

"Alright, boy," I hummed, hopping to my feet, leaves crunching beneath my weight. "Home we go."

Everything was as it should be.

Or so I thought until we made our way back to the path and I began searching for my basket.

It was nowhere to be found.

I frowned in confusion as I stared at the spot I had been sure I'd left it, scratching at my head beneath my hat while Rotho chased his tail unbothered. My fingers caught in a snarl. Ugh. That meant it was probably time for a haircut again. I'd been avoiding it.

I hated things like that.

Appearance things.

Thank God I'd been both blessed and cursed with my grandfather's genes and the fact that it was basically impossible for me to grow anything but a five o'clock shadow. I couldn't imagine how annoying it would've been to have to shave every day.

I'd thought I put the basket right there.

I felt like I was losing my mind.

With a sigh, I scrubbed my hand over the sandpapery texture on my cheeks before I decided it was best we cut our losses and head home.

I'd been too trusting.

Someone had clearly come and stolen my basket after all.

Most of my garden was almost ready to be picked. It had been a good season, and I couldn't wait to begin freezing, canning, and storing the bits I wouldn't be able to eat quickly enough. I tried to grow most of the food I ate myself, but there were still things I had a hard time making on my own, such as anything that required a stove.

I balanced my lack of cooking skills with my knack for baking bread. Baking and knitting were probably my only marketable skills, unless you counted having an insane amount of freckles or an almost suspiciously green thumb.

That day I'd celebrated the plentiful harvest with a pan of cornbread I'd eaten entirely on my own. Thoughts of my stolen basket haunted me as I stayed up later than I usually did, my belly full and warm, my imagination running wild.

There was something in the air.

Something new.

Anticipation had trickled with the wind through my window and I felt almost feverish from it. It was late out, far too late for me, really. I tended to rise with the sun, and normally I was in bed only minutes after the light had bled from the sky. Tonight, however, I was wide awake as I waited.

The walls of my cottage were lined with warm wood, plants hanging from every nook and cranny. Vines from my Pothos plant drooped between the hooks I'd inlaid in the walls, reaching toward the light, their leaves growing larger the longer they thrived indoors. Living inside what basically amounted to a greenhouse made me feel at peace in a way the buildings in town never did.

They were too clean, too structured, too impersonal.

In comparison my home was dirty, chaotic, and full of personality.

My heart thrummed as I curled up on my loveseat, facing the window with my knees tucked in tight, and the orange and cream blanket I'd knitted the previous winter bundled around my body. The plants were new. The couch was not. It was a wonder I still fit sitting in the same position I had as a little kid watching the moon rise from this exact spot.

I was over six feet tall now, and most of the people I talked to had to look up to meet my gaze. Which I *hated*. Because I hated eye contact in general. There was something about being tall that made people want to stare at you.

I didn't mind when they wanted to chat. I just wished they'd do it where I could listen and not have to participate. Sometimes, when I was feeling particularly lonely, I'd sit on one of the benches in the town square, and I'd listen to the bustle of the people walking around. Phone conversations, laughter, gossip. I learned things about their families, their friends, their hobbies without ever having to actually speak.

It was how I stayed in touch with society even though I'd chosen to be as far removed from it as possible.

Sitting alone I let the world blur by me, like a fish in a bowl.

There were a lot of things I could get away with as a child that I couldn't as an adult. People didn't enjoy a fish bowl man the way they loved an awkward kid. I'd become a peculiarity. Maybe the spot where I sat on the couch hadn't changed, but I had.

The moon was steadily rising and I curled up tighter, Rotho's furry body beside mine, his heavy head tucked atop my thigh as we waited together. He wasn't amused by the disruption to our schedule, and he kept giving me these judging looks that I couldn't help but find adorable despite him clearly being very serious about his displeasure. Maybe... if I was being honest, I hoped my basket would be returned like the first one had.

It was a crazy thought, truly. I'd already written off the first experience as coincidence, but still… my imagination ran wild.

The minutes ticked by, and my eyes drooped.

I could see my garden through the window, moonbeams decorating the thick tomato stalks, the leafy greens of my thriving squash, the swell of watermelons where they grew fat and ripe along their vines. It looked peaceful as it always did when blanketed by nightfall. It should've calmed me, but it didn't. Instead my hands shook, my heart raced, and my eyes stayed trained on the familiar shapes as new feelings threatened to overwhelm me.

Fear.

Suspense.

Excitement.

Only—apparently I was destined for disappointment. Because hours into my wait, nothing had happened.

Nothing.

When I awoke the next morning, I had a crick in my neck and that weird feeling of anticipation was swirling like a serpent in my stomach as I made my way into the yard to pick my tomatoes. Except… when I arrived, my basket in tow, the stalks were—

Empty.

What the hell?

I spun around, searching for evidence of an intruder, my head swimming as I scrounged the overgrown walkways and the dew-damp mud looking for footprints. But there was no trace of anything at all, and I eventually abandoned my search in favor of heading inside for my morning cup of tea.

Rotho was not bothered by this development. His tail thumped lazily, tongue lolling as he padded around, leaving his muddy paw prints smeared all over the kitchen tile. Confused and more than a little stressed, I sat with my head in my hands at my little dining room table and tried to figure out what could possibly have happened.

Farmer Jones.

It must've been Farmer Jones.

Maybe it was uncharitable of me to suspect my neighbor, but Farmer Jones had been my nemesis for years. Not that I'd ever done anything to him to deserve his animosity. In fact, his anger spanned two generations. He'd always disliked my Aunt and Uncle. He'd loudly proclaimed their ways of parenting outdated. He didn't appreciate that they'd built our cottage within sight of his farm, and he *really* didn't like the fact that half the time my vegetables turned out juicier and fatter than the ones he sold at the farmers' market all summer long.

You'd think it wouldn't matter, since I never intended to sell anything, but apparently it did.

Maybe it was a pride thing.

Everything was a competition in his eyes. He'd threatened me on more than one occasion, constantly paranoid that I'd start growing pumpkins. He seemed to think that if I did, I'd somehow also miraculously get the guts to join the Fall Festival produce competition and maliciously steal his spot as Sacrifice. The man had won for more than ten years in a row, you'd think he'd be tired of washing red paint out of his hair. He never was though.

He enjoyed the prestige, and the traffic to his farm, far too much for that.

So, with all the past abuse, it wasn't too far-fetched an idea that the pug-like man would've come stomping over here just to mess with the competition, despite it not being a competition at all.

The more I thought about it, the more it made sense.

Anger, such an unfamiliar emotion, burned bright hot inside my chest as I finished my cup of tea and added it to the growing pile in the sink with a quiet *clink*. I'd have to do dishes later, when I was less upset.

For now I'd go over to his farm—yes. I'd go over there and I'd confront him!

I would.

I stomped all the way into my bedroom, donned my usual pair of overalls and long-sleeved shirt, and… ran out of determination the moment I pulled a holey sock onto my left foot.

What was I doing?

Sitting there. One-socked. Staring at the crack in my bedroom wall and trying to figure out where the hell I'd gone wrong. This wasn't me. I wasn't the confrontation type. Ever. I couldn't remember the last time I'd voluntarily walked into a conflict, and I sure as hell wasn't going to start today.

What the hell had I been thinking?

That I'd suddenly grow the power to be confrontational overnight? I couldn't even get myself to fucking grow pumpkins despite wanting to for years—and prepping a patch every season. I wasn't about to start a fight over a handful of Roma tomatoes, no matter how juicy or delicious they were.

Sunlight streamed in through the windowpane and Rotho woofed from the other room, a soft little noise that made me smile and shook me out of my reverie. So what if Farmer Jones had stolen my produce? I'd just grow more. That didn't mean I wasn't going to investigate though.

I figured now that I wasn't sleep-addled I could check for footprints again.

Maybe I'd missed something?

The air was hot and humid as I stepped out my front door, Rotho's furry body weaving through my legs. I hardly ever went out the front, but I was on the hunt for clues as I scanned the dirt road for threats and nearly tripped over a wayward tomato.

Wait.

What the hell?

It took me a second to process what I was seeing.

Tomatoes.

All of them.

Shiny and trimmed, positioned in a neat little row that spanned the entirety of my ancient front porch. They gleamed in the morning light, and my jaw dropped as I stood stock still, stunned for a moment too long before I jumped into action.

Had Farmer Jones picked them for me?

Was this his way of apologizing for the years of antagonism?

Or a new way to mess with me?

I'd never heard of passive-aggressive tomato picking before. I didn't know what to make of it. Now that it was done however, there was nothing I could do but move forward. I had tomatoes to rescue, after all.

I shook away my thoughts, headed inside, and grabbed a basket.

The next morning, I woke with a giddy feeling bubbling inside my chest. After the basket and the tomatoes I suspected something was afoot. Maybe it was Farmer Jones or maybe… *Maybe—*

No.

No. Best not to think about that, no matter how excited I was.

Suddenly, I was a kid again, hunting for presents to unwrap under a well-lit tree, the paper strewn across the room like a candy-cane-colored battleground.

I checked the garden first, my cup of tea held tightly, the warm porcelain burning my fingertips as I checked plant after plant. The zucchini were nearly ready though they were depressingly normal. My rhubarb was fattening up after its rebirth this spring, and my onions looked nearly ready, as well.

Nothing amiss.

Until I saw the squash.

Once again, the plants were unharmed, but the vegetables were missing. That same fluttery feeling I'd woken up with burst through my body as I immediately followed the cobbled pathway around the corner of my cottage to the front step where I'd found the tomatoes the previous day.

Sunshine beat on the back of my neck. I'd forgotten my hat, but I hardly even noticed because the moment I saw a perfect line of squash spread evenly across brittle wood, a laugh burst right from my chest.

Someone was picking my crops for me. Why? I didn't know.

I packed the squash into a basket the same way I had the previous day with the tomatoes, my cheeks warm, sweat beading on my brow. Huh. Whoever had plucked the squash had even scrubbed away the little fuzzy prickles that usually decorated the freshly grown vegetables. That took a lot of attention to detail, as well as a lot of time.

This pattern continued for several more days. I'd stay awake as long as I could until I ultimately fell asleep, and in the morning one of my crops would be meticulously cleaned and set neatly aside for me, already harvested.

On the fourth night, I concocted a plan. A new plan. A *clever* one. A plan that involved a whole lot of caffeine—which I never drank—and a whole lot of determination. It would work, I was sure of it.

A man on a mission, I even went into town to procure what I needed. It was too hot out for Rotho to accompany me, and I hid behind the wide brim of my hat as I hunted around the general store, triumphant when I found them sitting in a neat little row in the drink aisle.

Energy drinks.

I'd heard of them, sure, but never had one before. I'd never felt the need until now. How many would it take? One, two—*seven?* Wanting to be prepared I piled my basket full and ignored the weird look Tom gave me at the cash register.

"Long night?" he asked, clearly amused.

"I hope so," I agreed, too giddy to care about my social awkwardness. Tom snorted and shook his head, muttering something under his breath that sounded suspiciously like "kids nowadays."

I figured my body would have no choice but to succumb to the caffeine if I drank enough of it, and I was bound and determined to catch Farmer Jones in the act. I still wasn't sure if I was going to thank him or ask him what the hell he thought he was doing.

And if it wasn't him? I'd still catch a glimpse of my midnight visitor. It was a win-win situation, no matter who I ended up spotting.

My walk through the woods on the way home was as pleasant as it had always been; though, I kept a suspicious eye out for the basket thief who clearly lurked.

Unsurprisingly, the most notable thing I saw the entire time was a squirrel who'd gotten caught under a log just off the path. When I hopped to the mossy grass to rescue it, I'd kept my basket full of drinks close, just in case.

Rotho greeted me at the door as he always did, and I let him outside to use the bathroom before I plunked myself down on the loveseat to wait. The Red Bulls in my hands were cold to the touch, and I clutched them tightly in my fists, ready to shotgun them the second I felt my eyelids grow heavy. The sun dropped low on the horizon, the world painted in pink and persimmon, and I began to droop.

No.

No, *no*.

I had a *mission*.

And it did not include passing out before I could catch my Secret Harvester in action. I popped the tabs open on two of the cans, the motion familiar despite it having been nearly ten years since the last time I'd had a carbonated beverage.

The drink tasted like acid and something that was probably supposed to resemble fruit, but I didn't care, pushing through my disgust as I downed both drinks and clutched at my blanket—ready to wait.

Except.

I didn't factor in the fact that caffeine would make me restless as hell. I couldn't keep my legs from bouncing or my hands from twitching, and soon enough, just sitting on the couch was too tedious to continue to do. So I began cleaning, scrubbing first the bathroom, then the kitchen. I scrubbed the pile of dishes that I'd neglected and mopped this week's scattering of muddy paw prints from the tile. I figured it was safe to move about for a while, since whoever was coming only seemed to appear far enough into the night that no matter how late I stayed up, I always missed them.

Caffeine was… terrifying.

When the house was spotless and every last one of my hundred and thirty potted plants had been watered, I flopped back onto the couch to wait once again. Sweat beaded on my brow and my cotton shirt clung to my chest as I stared at the rising moon, trembling with anticipation.

Rotho's snores echoed through the quiet cottage, soothing me with their familiarity. He lay snuggled in a ball on a pile of my coats I'd accidentally knocked off the coat rack, and I watched him kick his legs in his sleep, turn over, and resume snoring once again.

It was late.

Far later than I'd ever stayed awake before.

I wasn't tired.

I wasn't.

I—

I woke up with a start, realizing I'd drifted off some time around three in the morning. My eyes felt dry, my mouth a desert as I jolted upright and stared out the window toward where the moon painted my garden silver with its ethereal glow. I could see the forest's silhouette, stark against the starry skyline, and something inside my chest lurched as a feeling not unlike self-preservation rose to the surface.

Hold still, the voice whispered.

Don't move.

Patience.

I froze, my breath catching as I squinted blearily at the garden. My eyes tracked over the dark outline of roots and leaves I had memorized, tracing their familiar contours with affection I'd never felt for anyone but Aunt June, Uncle Ruth, and Rotho. The fairy lights in my garden glowed sweetly, unobtrusive almost like fireflies.

Just like always, at first, there was nothing.

Nothing but the wind, the moon, the stars, and my garden.

The leaves danced. The wind whispered.

I almost gave up.

And then I saw *it.*

Him.

Chapter Three

THERE WAS A large figure crouched between two of my zucchini plants, their leaves obscuring the bottom half of his body. He was tall. Lean. *Muscular*. I recognized him immediately as I stared at the broad span of his shoulders and the majesty of his antlers. They spiraled like branches toward the flickering of the stars above, a crown atop his unruly curls. Shrouded in darkness he looked regal, like the king of the forest behind him. Before when I'd seen him I'd been terrified. Now though? My heart fluttered so hard I felt *faint* and my hands began to quake for an entirely different reason.

Why was he here?

Why *me*?

There's a monster in the woods.
That's what the stories always say.

I held still.

My breath stuttered and my eyes burned. I refused to blink for fear of missing something as I watched him move, his long fingers graceful as he continued to meticulously pluck all the zucchini from their stems, his head bowed, face shadowed by the riotous flop of his hair.

He was real.

The monster was real.

Except… he didn't look particularly monstrous.

He looked… gentle.

Soft.

Focused.

If I wasn't watching it happen right in front of me, I wouldn't have been able to believe that he'd been the one harvesting my plants for me and the person who returned my basket after I'd left it abandoned in the woods. I'd rationalized for months that what I'd seen that day in the forest had been a fantasy. Now though? There was no denying that the monster was no fairytale.

He wasn't human, but he certainly wasn't what I'd thought he'd be either. There was an animalistic grace to his movements, while careful, he shifted that powerful body like a beast. Others might have seen him in the past, noted the lack of humanity, and dubbed him nothing but a dangerous predator, but as I observed him, curious amazement buzzing brightly at my fingertips, I came to the conclusion that he was so much more.

A monster that liked to garden.

I had to cover my mouth for a moment to stifle my giggle.

He reached for another zucchini, gingerly cradling it in his massive palm before he held it up to his face and *sniffed* it. I held back another laugh, too enthralled by his actions to do anything other than stare.

After he had sniffed along the fruit for a solid minute, a long, pink tongue flickered out from between his plump lips. My belly flipped. I squirmed, unable to help the way my mouth grew dry as the dexterous appendage—way too long to be human—stretched to tap at the outer edge of the zucchini with a sense of curiosity I could almost taste myself.

Fascinated, I trembled as the creature opened his mouth, revealing the gleam of a pearly white row of fangs before he sank his teeth into its flesh. The movement was so calculated, and quizzical I couldn't help but be charmed despite his long black claws and the vicious glint of razor-like teeth.

I could so easily imagine the sound it made. The crunch of the thick green outer skin breaking beneath the force of his bite, the burst of juice exploding along his longer than normal tongue, dripping from the corners of his lips onto the night-damp soil below.

I wondered if he liked the taste.

I wondered if he wanted *more*.

Was he the kind of creature that only partook in food of the flesh? From where I sat observing him, the answer was obvious.

He was open to experimentation.

The minute I sat there, twitching and hot as I hungrily observed him, felt far longer than it should've. No one had ever made me feel like this. Ravenous. Scared. Excited, all at once. His hair parted with the breeze and I was struck by the expression on his face as he crunched away thoughtfully, shock and a little amazement unfolding across the shadowy contours of his handsome features. Thank goodness I'd installed fairy lights along the back wall in my garden! Without them, I was sure I wouldn't have been able to see him in such clear detail.

He started to pluck again, snacking on his treat with one hand as he rustled through the bush, brow furrowed, eyes glowing with determination.

His forearms flexed and shifted, his claws flicking dexterously to sever the stems from the vine as moonlight highlighted the veins on the top of his charcoal colored hands.

I couldn't see his cock with the way he crouched, the bushes concealing it from view. It was a strange feeling, wanting to see someone else's dick. I'd never felt it before, not the way everyone made me think I should.

I'd never felt this burning desire, like lava coursing through my veins. His biceps tensed, growing somehow impossibly more defined, as he added to the growing pile at his side and I traced the contours of his thick chest with my eyes. He had *nipples*. Which shouldn't have felt like such a strange thing—but it did. They were pale and hard—probably because of the cold, and their presence only made him look even more human despite the obvious differences between us.

Everything was going well before the universe decided I'd ogled him enough and a sneeze began to tickle up the length of my throat. No, no, *no. I wasn't done.* I wanted to see more. I fought it off for as long as I could. Tears burned in my eyes and my nose tingled as I inhaled raggedly, lost my internal battle, and sneezed.

The sound was so loud that even Rotho jumped, glaring at me from where he had risen from his pile of discarded things, his brown eyes accusatory, his ears down. He'd distracted me.

The spell was broken.

When my gaze snapped back to the garden and the spot the creature had just occupied, he was gone, his figure nothing but a speck on the horizon as he disappeared into the woods once again.

The next morning, I had almost convinced myself the whole thing had been a caffeine induced fever dream. *Could you blame me? I mean, gardening monsters?* It didn't seem possible, even though I'd seen it.

It hadn't happened.

I was sure—

At least until I found my way into the garden as I always did, and spotted the pile of plucked zucchini. Sitting slightly away from the rest lay one wayward piece with a few big, toothy bites missing.

I panicked.

After a good hour of pacing around my kitchen, I finally managed to work through my existential crisis. By the time I was feeling settled once again, I had nursed three cups of tea and brought all the remaining zucchini inside to store in my fridge.

I brought the half-eaten piece too. Sat it on the counter, and stared at it while I worked, letting the razor sharp bite marks act as my compass to reality. I wasn't delusional. That much was obvious.

The monster was real.

He was real.

And, apparently, he liked my vegetables.

He liked gardening.

He was gentle enough not to scratch a single tomato, despite his frankly vicious looking claws.

He was the kind of monster who returned baskets when they were lost in the woods.

And while all these things were odd, the strangest fact of all, was that he knew where I lived in the first place. Had he followed me home? Why?

Just how long had he been watching me?

I wasn't sure how I felt about the whole thing as I went about my day, stroking Rotho's head for support even though I didn't appreciate the critical faces he kept making at me.

"Stop looking at me like that," I sighed as he pawed at the back door. "It's not as though I meant to scare him off."

He pointed his nose toward the woods, and I wasn't sure if it was the universe wanting to taunt me or if maybe, just *maybe*, Rotho sensed what I did.

That the creature was lonely.

That he was *kind*.

That he was seeking connection.

The next day as the sun rose high overhead—and my heart rose up my throat along with it—I hatched another plan. I was getting quite good at those. However, I'd need a basket for this to work. Unfortunately, I was running low, since *someone* had stolen my spare, so I headed into town to buy a new one.

Farmer Jones was inside the general store, and I steered clear of him as I always did, ignoring the familiar grating sound of his laugh as he flirted with the happily married cashier. I traipsed around the back wall, my hat pulled low, my fingers fumbling and clumsy as I felt along the shelf full of baskets, trying to find the very best one.

It was a meticulous process.

And I couldn't go by looks alone.

That would be shallow.

The basket needed to be functional, full of character, and carry good energy with it. Sometimes it was the ugliest basket of all that ended up being the one I took home. I tended to go through new baskets rather quickly, even when they weren't being stolen.

Humming softly under my breath as I worked, I stroked gently along the handles and the bottoms, testing the weight of each individual basket until I settled on what I knew to be the best of the batch.

Slightly lopsided.

Honey brown.

Perfect.

"Ellis. Planting pumpkins this year, I see." The voice startled me and I whipped around, my heart in my throat, the brim of my hat flapping as I promptly dropped the basket I'd selected and slapped a hand on my head to keep it on.

The basket!

Oh no.

I hadn't meant to drop it like that.

Quickly, I bent to pick it up, glaring at the familiar sturdy yellow work boots standing way too close to me because I didn't have the guts to glare outright at their owner. They were splattered with mud as they always were and paired with thick Levi jeans that had more holes than was probably recommended. And above the T-shirt-covered monster of a chest sat Farmer Jones's ruddy pink head.

He looked like an overripe tomato. Except, that would be an insult to tomatoes—so I took that back, immediately.

I grimaced, scowling at the corner of his mouth because looking him in the eyes only ever led to becoming far too overwhelmed to function for hours afterward. I could handle the chit chat of the other townspeople, and even the rumors, but Farmer Jones's outright hostility made my skin crawl.

"I haven't planted pumpkins," I told him. "I never do." *Not until next year*, I privately added. *Hopefully.*

"I beg to differ," he grunted, clearly peeved with me like he always was. I hadn't done anything to him, so I did my best to push aside the unease that his anger always caused. I brought my shoulders back, my fingers wrapped tight enough around the handle of my new basket that they turned white. I could feel indents from the weave knitting into my flesh as I squeezed, leeching as much strength as I could from the object in my grasp. The pain reminded me I was real. It grounded me, just as the soil and the feeling of dirt beneath my nails did.

"I think I know a pumpkin when I see one," Farmer Jones hissed.

"Well. Good for you." I ducked around him, confused and annoyed.

I was pretty damn sure I'd remember planting pumpkins. I'd thought about it, of course I had. But at this point I didn't have the guts to outright go against him.

That didn't mean I wasn't annoyed though.

What rankled me the most was the fact that he'd so clearly been on my property without my permission. No matter how misguided his attempt at heckling me was, he'd still invaded my privacy. Even if I *had* planted pumpkins he had no right to trespass.

My garden was my sanctuary.

Feeling violated, I clutched my basket, made my purchase, and fled.

On my way back through the woods, my anger and humiliation made it hard to breathe. I couldn't even muster the energy to be excited about my plan and my newest purchase. The familiar spread of branches overhead did nothing to cool the heat inside my heart as I stomped along the path, pebbles rolling and crunching underfoot.

I *hated* feeling like this.

I hated Farmer Jones.

Frustrated tears pricked at the corner of my eyes as I hurried home, desperate for the sanctity of my cottage and garden. Off to my left I heard a suspicious rustle, and instead of ignoring it and moving on like I normally would, I was too incensed from my encounter with Farmer Jones to stop the words from slipping from my lips.

"I don't know who or what you are," I said to the whistle of the wind as the leaves danced and the sun trembled high in the sky, "but it's rather rude to come to my home and not *at least* introduce yourself."

And with that, I stomped the rest of the way home.

That night I enacted my plan.

I regretted my rash words earlier as my anger hadn't been with the creature, but with a certain red-faced, dirty-booted, greasy-lipped menace. However, I figured at the end of the day there was no guarantee the creature had even been there at all, and if he *had*, there was a chance he didn't speak English, so it was possible he hadn't understood me at all.

Luckily for me, he didn't need to speak English to understand what a gift was.

And I owed the monster an apology and my gratitude for all the work he'd done in my garden.

That was why the plan had to continue, despite my earlier mistake. I just hoped he'd forgive me if he'd seen. I hoped that maybe he hadn't understood. That he wouldn't think less of me now, that he'd seen me at my worst.

I filled the basket I'd bought with rows of my best vegetables, plucked and primed by my new friend, polished clean by me. When the basket was full, it was as colorful as a May Day parade and looked absolutely delicious. I admired my work with a happy grin, pulling the basket off the table to show it to Rotho for approval.

"What do you think?" I hummed, watching the way his tail began to wag. "Do you think it's pretty enough for an apology basket?"

More tail wagging commenced, followed by a baleful look as Rotho padded toward his food bowl and pushed the empty container toward me with a huff and a sigh.

"You're no help." I squinted at him, amused by his dramatics, placing my basket on the table again before I headed over to fill his bowl. "At least not when you're hungry."

The moment it was full he went to town, the soft *crunch, crunch* soothing me as I returned to the table, my hands on my hips, inspecting my gift in the hopes I could picture what the monster would see when he looked at it.

I could almost smell the pollen and earth in the air surrounding it. Colorful. Beautiful. Vibrant. *Yes.* He'd like it. Probably, anyway. I hummed to myself, pleased, as I arranged the last of the vegetables then loaded it onto my arm.

Confident now, I strode down my front walkway and toward the edge of the forest where I'd seen the creature run off. Dirt crunched beneath my feet, pebbles digging through the thin soles of my worn sneakers. I spared a glance toward Farmer Jones's farm just up the road. Because of my earlier conversation with him I was a little on edge, expecting him to show up on my property again, armed with his own self-righteousness.

It felt less safe now that I knew he'd been here.

No one was supposed to come here.

Well, except the monster, but he was the exception to the rule.

Tall grass tickled at the pads of my fingertips as I stepped off the road and plodded my way through the field that separated my garden from the woods. The sun was about to set, the sky painted peach, and I heaved a great big sigh as I lay my basket down on top of a boulder at the very edge of the forest.

I could hear the small animals hidden beneath leaves and behind shadows chattering away like little gossips. The wind tickled my bangs, like a caress as I listened in amusement. Sometimes it felt like the creatures were whispering about me.

Here comes the boy again, they'd murmur.

The one with leaves in his hair.

The one that always smells like the sun and growing things.

The one who wears sun-kisses on his cheeks and dirt beneath his nails.

I readjusted the vegetables again, fixing the plants that had jostled out of place during my walk over till they all sat perfectly once again. The creak of tree limbs dancing above distracted me for only a moment before I took a step back to admire my work for the second time that day.

Lovely.

Yes.

I was sure he'd like it.

I nodded to myself, more than a little pleased.

The bright coloring of the fruits and vegetables made my basket stand out against the backdrop of dark tree trunks behind it and I hummed thoughtfully, delighted with how wonderfully everything had gone. Satisfied, I rose to my full height, stretching on the tips of my toes to better squint into the darkness between the trees.

Maybe *he* was there.

Maybe *he* was listening.

Maybe I was crazy after all.

"If you can hear me, I just want to say that I'm sorry for what I said earlier," I called into the darkness, very aware that in that moment I looked as unstable as everyone always said I was. "It was rude of me. I don't understand your culture, but for humans we typically like a polite hello before we begin harvesting each other's gardens." I blinked, squinting harder as I listened to rustling in the leaves again, and I waited for some sort of response.

Nothing came.

So, like an idiot, I spoke again.

"I've brought you a gift. I didn't mean to startle you the other day. I was just surprised to see you. But I appreciate all you've done for my garden, and I figured you deserved a taste of your hard work."

Still nothing.

I wasn't sure what I'd expected, considering the fact he never left the woods before nightfall. Sighing, I slumped, grabbing the top of my hat so it wouldn't fly off as the wind caressed my flaming cheeks almost in apology and I turned back home. Alone.

The next day I found the most unexpected gift on my doorstep.

A bottle of strawberry rhubarb jam. My favorite kind. *Huh.* I blinked at it in confusion, twisting to look toward the woods curiously. Scanning the field hungrily, I searched in the direction I'd left my gift basket in the evening before for clues. Nothing was amiss, and the basket was gone.

Which didn't surprise me.

The jam did, though.

It didn't take a genius to figure out that this was the exact bottle of jam I'd bought at the general store all those weeks ago. It seemed my monster thieved baskets as often as he returned them. Funny that he'd liked my gift enough he'd decided to give me a gift of his own. I hid my smile, embarrassed by how happy that simple gesture made me.

"Thank you!" I called, feeling once again like a loon as I reached down to grab the cool glass jar. Rotho burst through the door behind me, bounding past, to frolic in the morning mud. I watched him for a minute, laughing as he flopped onto his back and folded his upper legs in a way that meant he was demanding belly rubs.

Silly human, it won't pet itself, his eyes seemed to say. I had no choice but to comply, mud be damned. I cradled the jam close to my chest as I crouched beside him, my fingers sinking into damp, gritty, tangled fur. Something warm fluttered its wings deep inside me, unfurling like a caterpillar escaping its cocoon.

The woods waved in the wind, and my heart burst as excitement for the future nearly overwhelmed me.

For a week the pattern continued.

Every morning I'd wake up and a new item from my missing basket would appear on my porch in perfect condition. And every time I saw the new gift, I had to hold back my laughter as I called out my thanks to the trees, imagining the monster lurking in the shadows as he waited to see my reaction. I wasn't sure why he did what he did. There was something deeper behind the action, that I couldn't seem to understand no matter how hard I tried.

Maybe in his culture the gifts meant something different.

Or maybe he was lonely.

Maybe he craved connection.

A friend.

Maybe monsters needed companionship just like humans did, I mused to myself as I packed away the most recent gift of blackberry syrup. Due to the summer heat, the liquid inside the bottle had separated, and I shook my head in disbelief as I brought it inside, unable to help the smile that spread across my lips.

I didn't think I could eat it now, but the sentiment was nice.

He was sweet, in a primitive sort of way. He couldn't go into the village to buy me gifts, so he was being inventive. I appreciated the effort.

Rotho nipped at my heels and I laughed, hopping out of the way as I slid into my seat at the dining room table and pulled my knees up so I was sitting cross-legged. It was hard to fit into such a small space, but I managed, just as I always had. The wood creaked beneath my weight as I stared at the floral pattern on the wall and mulled over whether or not he'd like what I had planned next.

Rotho brushed along my bare legs and I reached down absentmindedly to pat at his head, stroking behind his ears, because I knew it was his favorite. His back leg thumped happily, his tongue lolling as I judged the new basket sitting on the table in front of me with a critical eye. I needed to finish arranging it. I wanted it to be perfect. Though I'd begun the process the night before, it still felt unfinished. This time, instead of my typical offering of vegetables, I'd packed it full of something I considered of even higher value.

Bread.

My signature loaves. The ones my Aunt and Uncle had devoured every time I made them. I'd spent the entire previous day baking loaf after loaf—cinnamon, garlic and herb, cheese, and wheat. Each loaf was browned to perfection, fluffy in the center, with a crust that scraped *just right* when I dragged the flat end of my knife across it to test its texture.

I figured it might crunch satisfyingly enough under even monster teeth. I hoped, anyway. *I wanted him to like it.* Though, I wasn't sure if monsters enjoyed bread.

Meat, sure.

Vegetables? Apparently.

But bread?

I suppose I was about to find out.

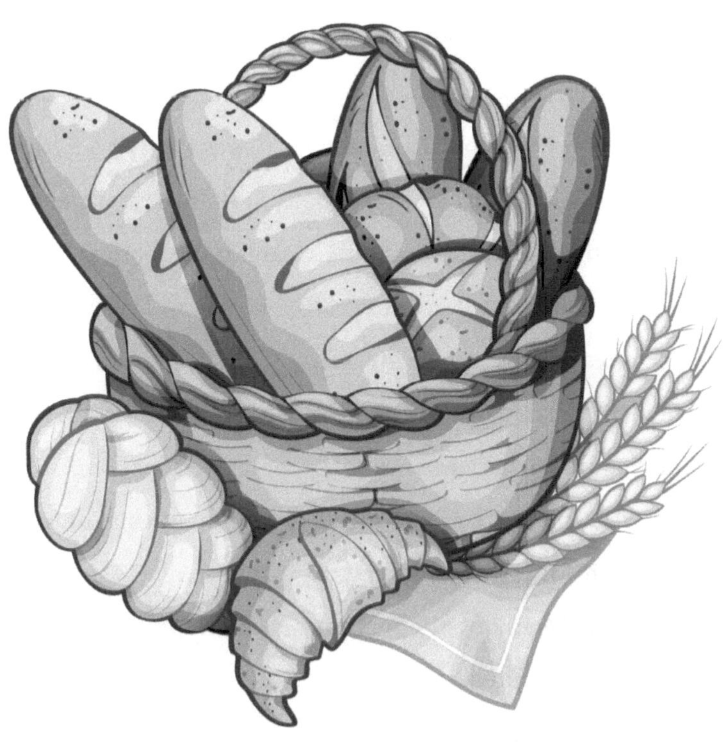

Chapter Four

THAT NIGHT I lay in wait, the lights off, an empty can of Red Bull clutched in my grip. I sat on the couch, body tense, as the silver moon rose, and the stars above appeared one by one like pinpricks of paint splattered carelessly across the inky sky. The forest was a far-off beacon of hope outside my window. In hindsight, it was funny how frightened I'd been of it just a few short months ago. Even funnier, however, was the fact that before then, I hadn't thought much about the forest at all. Now it was all I could think about. More accurately, *he* was all I could think about.

As the trees danced, so did my heart.

Excitement buzzed against my ribs like a hummingbird's wings, and I stroked behind Rotho's ears, seeking comfort. *Thump, thump* went the steady beat of his heart as my fingers caught on a patch of dried mud in his downy brown fur, and I picked my way through it, always gentle. Big brown eyes flickered questioningly at me as I tipped my head toward the moonlight and I waited.

And waited.

And waited.

And waited.

I sat there until my eyes drooped and the clouds that spread across the starry skyline faded into a vague, sleepy blur. *Defeat.* That's what this sinking, horrible feeling was. I should've never allowed myself to get this excited, not when I hadn't known if the monster would ever come back.

All day I'd imagined his response—and I could admit now, drowsy and a little heartbroken, that I'd been foolish to think he'd return. My basket of bread lay abandoned at the edge of the garden near the empty pumpkin patch. I'd stared at it for so long I wasn't even sure it was real anymore. It had become nothing but a hazy, blobby smudge as I squeezed my eyes shut and fought off my disappointment.

He wasn't coming.

Rotho nuzzled my hand with a quiet little grunt and I sighed, burying my face in his fur as I gathered my wits again and decided what to do. I couldn't just leave the bread to the elements. It'd only been a few hours, it would probably still be edible if I brought it in now. If I waited, the morning dew would seep inside its crust and ruin it. So even though I was exhausted and disheartened, I rose dejectedly from my comfortable seat on the couch and strode across the dusty floor toward the back door.

The screen whined on its hinges like it always did as I gently pushed it open. I could fill a Rolodex with childhood memories slamming through that door, and into the open air. Season after season, the hinges would screech the same, no matter how old I became. The memories faded as quickly as they'd come, disappearing into the blanket of night as Rotho side-eyed me from where he'd plopped himself behind me in the middle of the kitchen tile.

It's too late for us to go out, his eyes said. *Shouldn't you be in bed?*

Sometimes he was more like an old man than I was. Not that either of us were particularly qualified to wear that moniker. Him being a dog and me being—well, whatever it was, I was.

A hopeless romantic maybe?

Lonely, my brain supplied unhelpfully.

The moment I stepped outside, the sound of crickets tickled my eardrums and the sweet scent of the summer air swelled inside my nose. Warmth expanded through every pore in my body as the comfort of the outdoors gave me peace once again. It was hard to be sad when the air was this fresh and the breeze tugged at my curls to cheer me up.

Becoming one with the shadows, I slipped across the broken cobblestones, my bare feet dusted with dirt and bits of broken earthen-things. I paused and brushed my toes along the contours of the cement block in the middle of the pathway that housed my childhood hand and footprints inside it. I wished, not for the first time, that my Aunt June and Uncle Ruth had made a matching one all those years ago.

I hadn't anticipated them leaving me so soon.

Though, I supposed they must be happy now, reunited with the earth as June had always hoped to be.

My toe caught at the edge of five-year-old Ellis's handprint and I frowned, the sorrow I always felt when thinking about them welling up inside me once again. It would've been nice to see their handprints here, ten years after their deaths, buried in the dirt. Maybe it would've made it easier to remember Aunt June's smile, or the way Uncle Ruth always smacked her on the ass with his dirty gloves when she'd stood, her knees creaking from kneeling in the garden all day. Maybe I would've been able to recall her laughter more clearly, or the taste of her famous pumpkin soup. Or the way she'd made me feel, loved and whole, perfect with all my imperfections.

I shoved my hands into the pockets of my overalls and sighed at the empty field separating my home from the wild, my eyes dry, my chest aching. It was hard to be sad outside when it was this beautiful, but it wasn't impossible.

Why hadn't he come?

I reached for Rotho's soothing presence, my fingers ready to bury in his fur, only to be met by the caress of a breeze and nothing but empty space. *Right.* He hadn't followed me out. He was probably laying by the screen door, asleep, waiting for me to return. I put my hand back in my pocket, swallowing around the lump in my throat.

I couldn't help my disappointment as I pushed open the rickety gate that separated my garden from the rest of the wild things and my feet sunk into the soil. It clung to me like a well-worn glove and I loosened my muscles, letting my lungs expand and my heart relax, my head tipped toward the moon, where its glow spread thin through the gossamer fog of clouds overhead.

It had been so long since I'd been out at night like this.

I'd forgotten how peaceful it was.

Like the world had been reclaimed by its rightful owners and nature was queen again.

I was quiet, as I always was. But the silence felt less oppressive than it did when I was in town, surrounded by the bustle of people and the chatter of inconsequential things. Everyone was always in a hurry there. As much as I liked the ambiance of the city's idle gossip, being alone out here at night was far different than being alone on my usual bench in the middle of the town square.

Here, the only gossips were the chatty owls at the edge of the wood.

I crouched when I reached the spot where I'd left the basket at the edge of the field. My disappointment still felt prevalent though faded, as I fingered the handle. What the hell did I think I was doing? Truly?

Feeding a monster?

Befriending it?

Did monsters even *have* friends?

A voice echoed in the back of my mind, and I pushed it aside even though the words remained despite my protests.

Was he even a monster at all?

As I plopped into the dirt, a whisper of a cool breeze tickled my cheekbone, lifting and twisting my flop of curls in its gentle caress. The wind once again greeted me like an old friend and I sighed, scrubbing a hand over my face.

Wait—

What was that?

Rotho howled, a quiet sound that echoed through the cracked open windows. I froze, my heartbeat stuttering to life. *Thud, thud, thud.* My body trembled.

Rotho *never* howled.

Ever.

Something was happening.

I raised my head, the hair on my arms rising as my heart performed a ballet in my chest. It thrummed and throbbed with a slow-building anxiety I couldn't help but compare to the feeling of dipping my toes in cool creek water. Sharp. Familiar. Startling, all the same.

That was when I saw him.

A broad-shouldered, familiar shadowy figure approached, his willowy frame blending in with the trees behind him as he stepped gracefully outside of the forest. His long legs slipped between the blades of grass but there was no sound aside from the whisper of the wind. Naked and gorgeous, his thighs flexed and his soft cock shifted from side to side with every careful step he took. His ebony claws glinted when they caught the light, a gorgeous smattering of dark hair trailing from his belly button down to his frankly massive dick.

I couldn't look away.

This was not like the other times I'd encountered him. Before I'd been hidden, with trees or walls to separate us. I couldn't be sure he'd ever truly spotted me at all. Now though? There were no barriers.

He could see me.

He could see me, and yet he didn't turn away.

My breath caught as he continued to close the distance between us. Stuttering, stuttering, stuttering—my heart threatened to escape my chest as adrenaline coursed through my blood. *Run.* That's what my body was telling me: *run before his talons meet your flesh and your soul is separated from your body.*

I didn't run, though. I stayed kneeling, exactly where I was. I could feel the exact moment the tension in my body began to soften, as those glowing yellow eyes met mine, and the creature cocked his head to the side—like a giant, curious cat.

Maybe I stayed because I was brave, maybe I was simply stupid.

Or maybe, *just maybe*, deep down the creature sensed what I did. That we were two ships at sea, our paths crossing in an anomaly that would rewrite our course for the rest of time.

The fairy lights I'd placed around the garden wall behind us lit up his antlers as they climbed toward the clouds, shrouded in pale moonlight. His overgrown curls obscured the vast majority of his face, but I still recognized the angular shape of his nose and his generous lower lip. The closer he became the easier it was to make out the small details: his collarbones, his Adam's apple, the exact shade of ebony at the tips of his fingers and toes as it transitioned to meet tanned, sun-kissed skin.

I'd never been so enraptured by someone before, so stunned, so… floored.

Step by step, he prowled through the grass, the hoot of owls in the trees, and the chirp of crickets blanketing his approach.

He was silence. He was strength. He was the earth itself—the grass parting respectfully before his footsteps like he was its king.

Sweat gathered at my temples and along my chilled palms where they rested tentatively on the handle of the basket I held. It was slightly damp from nervous sweat now. I flexed my fingers, clutching it tight as I slowly, *slowly*, rose to my feet to greet him.

And then he was there, right in front of me.

Everything was still.

Tranquil.

Even the fireflies that lit up the valley had frozen as the creature stepped in close, his long bare limbs pulled taut with sinewy muscle and the flicker of blue-black veins. He smelled of summer breezes, spring rain, and autumn wind—the crisp chill at the beginning of winter, fallen leaves, and August heat.

His scent tingled on my tongue, and I tipped my head back so he could look at me, though I had yet to find the courage to outright meet his gaze. Even now, I struggled with eye contact. Which was frustrating, considering the fact that his attention made my blood sing. He was *staring.* I could feel his gaze like a caress on my body.

You're acting like a weirdo, Ellis, I chided myself. *Move!*

With shaking hands, I held the basket out between us—an offering—our silence louder than words. He loomed over me, taller than I remembered. Or maybe, because I'd never gotten this close, I hadn't realized just how large he actually was. For most of my life, I'd been the tallest person in the room no matter where I was, but standing beside him, I shrank.

Without his antlers, I guessed he had to be over seven feet tall. *With* them, he was maybe eight, or nine? My belly flipped at the thought. I'd never thought I'd like feeling small, but I did.

The slope of the creature's nose was as generous as his full lips, as he tipped his head curiously to the side for the second time that night, and my breath escaped in a punched-out *woosh.* Did he not understand that I was giving him the food? Maybe I should explain.

"I thought you might like this," I said softly, my hands wobbling, muscles burning, as I continued to hold the basket out. The loaves of bread looked woefully flat without the sun to lend them color. I wished suddenly that I'd thought to bring a flashlight or something. He probably didn't understand what I was giving him. I had a feeling he'd never eaten cooked food before; maybe to someone who usually feasted on raw meat, bread didn't look appetizing at all. "I... like the presents you've been leaving," I told him with a smile. I wasn't sure if he understood me, and I hoped if nothing else, he'd understand my intent.

Maybe making him bread hadn't been my best idea. What if he didn't like it?

Was it mushy now? Dear God, don't let it be mushy.

My heartbeat skittered, and my legs trembled in a way I'd never felt before as I held my breath for what felt like an eternity, anticipating his response. Finally, he moved—silent and deliberate. His long, blackened talons glinted as he reached out and gingerly held the basket in his grip. I could still feel the heavy caress of his gaze as his hand lay beside mine, just inches away.

I couldn't bring myself to let go, terrified he'd leave the moment I gave it over. Instead I stared. His hands were massive. Both in length and width. Veins danced along his flesh—and there was something so effortlessly masculine about the way he squeezed the basket gently, careful not to break it even though he easily could. I swallowed the lump in my throat as his sculpted chest rose and fell with every breath. They came quickly enough I wondered if he was as nervous as I was.

Probably not.

I couldn't hurt him the way he could hurt me.

Why would I make him nervous?

There was no denying that the creature was so much *bigger* than I was, so much stronger, so much deadlier—every movement he made had to be calculated. A surprisingly peaceful killing machine.

We were so different, but we had similarities as well.

While he was clearly an animal of some sort, there was a human side to him too. I stared at his hands—so normal looking—where he tentatively held the basket. If they weren't pitch black, if he didn't have razor-sharp talons, if he wasn't what felt like nearly twice my size—he could've passed for human.

Unlike the kind of people I'd spent my life avoiding, he didn't get angry that I didn't look at him. He was patient. He acted as though *I* was the frightened wild animal, not him. It was that passivity that gave me the courage to move. I wasn't sure how long we'd been standing there staring at each other.

I didn't want him to leave.

I wanted to…

I wanted to look at him—*truly*, look. It would be worth the discomfort. It had to be.

A weight lifted from my shoulders as I tipped my head to meet his gaze through the dark swathe of his fringe. I'd never liked eye contact. *Never.* But this didn't feel uncomfortable the way it always had in the past. It was a wonder I found the need to seek this now after a life full of torturous stares and avoidance.

But I did.

And it didn't hurt the way it normally did when I was forced to look into other people's eyes. He took the pieces of me I handed over with easy acceptance, genuine intelligence flickering in the amber glow of his gaze as he nodded his head. I finally forced my grip on the basket to slacken enough that he could take all of its weight if he wanted to. Despite my calluses, despite my suntan, despite the freckles, my hand looked tiny, delicate, *soft* where it laced around the handle beside his.

Why wasn't he taking it?

Hopefully he doesn't notice how bad my hands are shaking.

"I'm running out of baskets," I told him, breaking the silence, "so if you wouldn't mind returning this one, I'd really appreciate it."

He cocked his head the other way, the shadow that slanted beneath the swell of his full lips shifting as he seemed to contemplate this. Then he nodded, and something bright and eager burst free in my chest.

He understood me.

He understood me!

"Have you ever had bread before?" I asked, my heart in my throat, the crickets that sang in the garden bursting to life the moment my heart began to beat again.

He shook his head and I laughed, bright and happy. "You'll like it," I promised. "I *hope*, anyway," I added a little self-consciously.

He lifted his other hand, stroking along the edges of the top loaf with a thoughtful, curious expression. *Big hands. Very, big hands.* My cheeks burned. If I moved my hand even an inch we'd be touching. Maybe that thought shouldn't have made me as weak-kneed as it did. There was a catlike quality to his movements, more animal than man, but just as intelligent. Like he'd retained the nature of the wild, but his consciousness had evolved to understand human thoughts.

It was baffling to witness.

"Do you have a name?" I asked, and then, because I was stupid, I blurted out, "I'm Ellis."

He twisted his head inquisitively to the side in the opposite direction again, brow furrowed as he seemed to mull over this new information. Back and forth, back and forth. His fingers grew still where they wrapped around the loaf. He released it, then finally took the basket from my grip, promptly sitting in the dirt.

I'd assumed he'd head off into the woods to eat, so I was more than a little happy that he'd decided to stay after all.

I sat as well because it seemed rude not to, all things considered. My hands were empty, so I shoved them into my lap to keep them from trembling, watching him with rapt attention as he nestled the basket into the cradle of his thick naked thighs.

I can't see his dick anymore.

I shook that thought away, confused by my own disappointment.

It might be nice to invite him inside? But no. *No.* He might not fit through the door considering how tall his antlers were. Logistics. I didn't want to embarrass him the first time we truly talked. Later, I'd invite him. After I'd figured out which kind of bread he liked best.

Honestly, it was hard to wrap my head around the fact that I was seriously considering inviting the monster into my house in the first place. Maybe I *was* as weird as everyone seemed to think I was.

Why wasn't he eating?

Did he not understand that what was in the basket was food?

The dirt was damp, and the chill seeped through my overalls. I shuffled to get comfortable, less than three feet away from the creature I'd been fantasizing about. He was as fascinated with me as I was with him. His lips thinned and he huffed softly, making a contemplative expression before he seemed to come to a conclusion about something. When he raised a long-fingered hand and reached tentatively toward me, I held incredibly still, terrified of his claws. With his hand hovering just a few inches away, he observed my expression and waited for permission to touch.

Why did he want to touch me?

Maybe he saw me the way I saw Rotho—as something precious and soft to protect. I liked the thought as much as it bothered me. I didn't want to be his pet. I wasn't sure what I wanted, at least not yet. I was, however, as curious as he was.

This was wild.

This was all so wild!

My head spun, and I gave a barely perceptible nod before he relaxed his broad bare shoulders. As I waited, my heart skittering, I did my best not to stare too obviously at his pecs when they flexed and shifted, or the smattering of hair between his nipples. Scant centimeters remained between us, and I held my breath as he leaned closer, and finally, *finally* his fingers brushed gently against the fragile skin of my left cheek.

Fireworks shot up my spine the moment our skin touched and I gasped, shocked by the electrifying sensation. That was new—very new. *What the hell?* He stilled for a moment before he deemed the noise inconsequential, and his hand closed like a blindfold over my eyes.

The brush of his palm against my eyelids reminded me of what it felt like to sink into cool lake water in the early spring. A flutter of ice skittered through my veins as a popping sensation echoed in my ears, and suddenly the world grew blissfully silent.

Silent that was, until I heard *it*.

A whisper on the wind, the voice so quiet I had to strain myself to hear.

My name is Styx, it murmured.

You have entered my forest.

You have accepted my gifts.

And now, you are mine.

I swallowed, my heart skipping a beat as he released me and I opened my eyes. Cool air filled my lungs as I sucked in a breath, and I realized, belatedly, I'd forgotten to breathe. Styx was still looking at me, a thoughtful expression on his face as he retreated back to his side of the basket and I rubbed my sweaty hands on my thighs. My skin tingled where he'd touched me. His voice echoed in my head.

This didn't feel real.

Any of it.

"You can speak?" I asked, because that seemed like the most prevalent question. Styx shook his head, the movement minute but definite. "Communicate, then?"

He ignored me in favor of grabbing a loaf out of the basket and giving it a thorough sniff. It must've smelled appetizing because the next thing I knew he was slipping his long pink tongue between his lips and stroking along the crust in an exaggerated glide. My dick twitched, and I was so surprised by my instantly lustful reaction I nearly flinched.

Styx's nostrils flared and his glowing predatory gaze snapped immediately to where I'd *attempted* to casually hide my crotch. He cocked his head to the side, eyes narrowing thoughtfully before he deliberately stuck his tongue out again just to watch me blush. When he closed his mouth, he looked far too pleased with himself.

A few seconds ticked by as I waited, unsure what he was about to do next.

Styx's eyes were heavy and syrupy sweet, as anticipation danced in the air between us. *Was he enjoying this?* He looked like he was. With a playful glint in his eyes, Styx stuck out the pointed tip of his tongue and deliberately stroked along the loaf's crust in an exaggerated slide—slow and slippery. Up close like this, there was no denying that it was longer than a human tongue, *sharper*, slicker. It dripped with the glimmer of something that looked shinier and slipperier than spit.

My cheeks burned and I shifted uncomfortably, my stomach flipping as Styx sniffed the air again and whatever he found made his eyes darken while he stared directly at me.

This time, when his tongue slid back inside his mouth it made a frankly filthy, wet little noise. I *jumped.* In response, his lips curled into a predatory grin, like he knew something that I didn't. There was nothing human about his expression. His smile was long, and wide, and *all teeth.* His pale eyes were nearly black, fangs glistening. And staring at him, looking wild and wicked, painted by moonlight, I realized I had never seen anything more riveting in all my life.

Styx ate all the bread.

All of it.

In a single sitting.

I was still happy he hadn't taken off into the woods to eat alone like I'd expected. Instead, he sat within sneezing distance, cross-legged and naked, his antlers framing the moon between them. Enraptured, I couldn't help but stare as he devoured the entire basket, loaf by loaf, emitting little grunts and growls, clearly happy to savor one of my only God-given skills.

He offered me some of the garlic and herb loaf, but I politely declined, trying not to be affected by the way he positively devoured it. *Stop staring, Ellis,* I internally chided myself. Yet, I couldn't tear my eyes away; I was utterly fascinated. Those big shiny teeth tore into the crust—*crunch, crunch, crunching*—while crumbs spilled, and delight lit him up from the inside out. I had never been this happy just watching someone eat. The manner in which he ate was… sinful in a way. Pure pleasure. Carnal. Deliberate. *Delicious.*

Fireflies gathered in his hair like fairies and he smiled when he finished the last loaf, covered in crumbs and beautiful in all his feral glory.

Satisfied.

By the time the sun rose, Styx had to leave again, and I collapsed in bed, ignoring Rotho's judgmental gaze as my sleepless night caught up to me, and my blankets tangled around my muddy feet. I'd need to do laundry later, but I figured a little dirt never hurt anyone.

When I awoke, I enjoyed my usual cup of Earl Grey. It was nearing sundown once again, the sky doused in red with its daily farewell as I sank my knees into the dirt and I stared at the indent that Styx had left in the soft soil the night before.

When I escaped to my bedroom in a desperate attempt to get my sleep schedule back on track, I collapsed onto the still dirty sheets and tried not to think of him. I tried not to think about how much larger than me he was or the way his eyes lit up. I tried not to think about his massive hands, his wicked grin, or how strangely appetizing his cock had looked where it lay nestled in a tantalizing patch of dark unruly curls.

I tried, but I didn't succeed.

Would he taste salty—of sweat and earth? Would it feel good—to close my mouth around him—to suckle and savor? Would he grunt and growl the way he had when he was devouring the bread I'd baked? Would he grab my hair?

Would he like it?

Would he like me?

For the first time in as long as I could remember, I didn't ignore my dick as it strained eagerly against my boxers. Instead, I shoved my hand beneath the fabric, curled my fingers tight around the base and squeezed.

"Oh," I whimpered, surprised by how good it felt. The skin was spongy and warm as I ran my palm up the length of my shaft, teasing along the velvety vein that ran its length as I squirmed and gasped.

Through the open window I could hear the chirp of crickets. There was a rustle just outside, but I ignored it. My skin tingled as I remembered the way it felt when Styx's eyes were on me. He stared at me like I was something precious, something miraculous.

"Nhgh." I tossed my head back, panting as I rubbed my callused palm along the already sloppy, wet crown of my cock. It throbbed, a fresh burst of precum slicking the way as I dragged my fist down and began to tug with determination.

Those eyes.

Predatory.

Dark.

Light.

Both, at the same time.

Would he devour me as vigorously as he'd eaten the bread I made him? And that tongue—dear, God, that tongue. It was so long—and lovely—pink, slick, and dexterous. How would it feel if that wrapped around me? If he squeezed—if he—oh, oh, *oh!*

I came all over my fist with a quiet sob, my entire body quaking as a cool breeze escaped through the open window and stroked along the feverish swell of my cheek. I hadn't meant to think about Styx like that, but now that I had, I couldn't bring myself to feel guilty.

He never needed to know.

And if I drifted off to sleep immediately after, cum-covered, and content—there was no one there to judge me except the friendly wind and my own bewildered thoughts.

As I harvested the rest of my vegetables, I sighed wistfully, scrubbed the sweat from my brow, and wondered what would happen now. I'd seen too much to be able to convince myself that Styx was an illusion.

My imagination was creative but not creative enough to have made him up. I wasn't sure what to make of these new feelings. I'd always been terrified of unfamiliar things. Part of me hated the way my dick perked up whenever I thought about too sharp fangs and a too-long, slick pink tongue. I'd spent way too long picturing what Styx could do with something that long… that *flexible.* Those thoughts made me feel conflicted every time they arose, especially after what I'd done the night before in bed.

I'd always thought I was rather regular in that regard. I had sex every so often to sate the need, and I'd never been particularly picky. After a few uncomfortable encounters in town, I'd learned early on that sleeping with people I often interacted with only bred trouble. That was why in recent years, I'd decided sex wasn't worth the hassle after all.

I'd always found attraction strange. Where others seemed to bring emotion into the physical realm, I'd never been able to do that. The more sex I had, the less I understood the appeal—and the less I wanted to.

Women flocked to me almost as much as men did. But the conversation before and after the act was tedious at best—downright *painful* at worst. They didn't understand why I didn't want to be touched after we'd finished. They didn't understand that, for me, flirting meant digging my hands in the soil and inhaling the perfume of fresh life. I found no joy in sharing shallow commentary about physical attributes that I had no control over. I had never cared to keep track of how many people had praised the toffee color of my eyes, my ass, or the muscles I'd built toiling away in the garden.

I had never cared what any of them thought about me.

Maybe that was why my attraction to the monster made sense.

He was as wild as I had always felt I was, but *freer*, without the shackles of the general population's judgment clouding his decisions. He could be whatever he wanted to be. When trees were your only friends, there was no such thing as being superficial.

I envied that.

I envied *him*.

Rotho woofed at me and I laughed, rising from my crouch, my now full basket of produce clutched tightly in my grip. It was the same basket I'd used the night before and I couldn't help but imagine where Styx's fingers had wrapped around the handle. He'd been so much larger than I was. The phantom memory of fingers much longer than my own made me flush.

"I'm coming," I reassured him, letting the dirt sink into the knees of my overalls as I reached with my free hand to shield my eyes from the sun. I squinted out at the vague shape of the forest before me and imagined the creature looking back.

What did he see when he looked at me?

Did he like that my hair resembled the dry autumn soil? Did he like my freckles, born from days spent working beneath the summer sun? Did he appreciate the sturdy build of my shoulders or the way my fingers were stained with the remnants of earth, my nails always full of reminders from my last crop?

I'd always been told I was handsome. That I had long legs. That my hair was thick enough for girls to envy and for men to want to sink their fingers into. But none of that had mattered to me until now.

I wanted him to like those things about me.

I wanted him to like *me*.

Confused, I slipped back inside the house, Rotho tight on my heels.

Chapter Five

FARMER JONES'S PUMPKIN patch was bursting to life with workers. When fall hit, he'd turn his cornfield into a maze like always, and his pumpkins would be proudly displayed at the entrance with a hefty price tag. I could both see and hear the farmhands from my front porch as I nursed my morning cup of tea a week later. I sat on the bottom step with my bare feet buried in the dirt, enjoying the way the summer heat had dwindled into nearly nothing.

Rotho's head was heavy and warm on my thigh, his eyes imploring as his tail swayed in a steady *thump, thump* against the ancient wood.

He thought I had treats, even though I'd already told him twice that I didn't.

He was a dreamer though.

Optimistic.

My head was in the clouds as it often was, though this time for entirely different reasons. I wasn't thinking about pumpkin fields, avoiding people, or how to best utilize my garden space for next year. Instead, I thought about a long, slick tongue, a wicked smile, and eyes so pale they looked like sweet corn.

Styx had visited again.

And again.

And again.

He'd come so frequently I'd begun to expect him now. Like clockwork, around three in the morning, his limber silhouette would appear at the edge of the forest; though, unlike before, I didn't sit inside the safety of my home to witness it.

Every time he came, I greeted him at the border of my garden, the stars dancing above us as he twisted his head curiously to the side, his eyes twinkling with mirth. Each visit he brought me a new gift. He'd run out of items from the basket he'd pilfered, so he'd started to find me things instead: a handful of glossy acorns, an armful of wildflowers, a crown made of flexible green branches. The moment he handed me something new, he'd regard me with eager anticipation, waiting for my reaction.

After the first couple visits, it'd been easier and easier to act normal around him. Though, admittedly, it hadn't always been so effortless. The second night Styx had visited had been painfully awkward at first.

After the pleasure I'd taken while thinking of him, I hadn't known how to react when he reappeared. I'd felt two sizes too big for my own skin as his tongue slipped along the piece of celery I'd given him, a thoughtful look on his face. He had a surprising talent for making any and all vegetable consumption look pornographic.

I certainly wasn't complaining.

Apparently he wasn't either.

The nerves quickly went away when I realized he *liked* the way I looked at him. I could see it in the way his eyes darkened, in the way he deliberately repeated each motion he discovered got a rise out of me. The more I blushed and stammered, the more pleased he became.

He was always learning.

Teasing.

I was territory he had yet to map out, and I was enjoying every last one of his explorations. I liked his attention. I liked it a lot. From that point onward, everything between us had been effortless. He would fluster me, I would enjoy it, our friendship growing stronger with every visit to the cottage he made.

It hadn't taken long for Styx to figure out that his tongue was the most tantalizing weapon he possessed, and he used it to his advantage whenever possible. It was a little embarrassing how quickly he'd figured me out.

We were at the precipice of something… new, though neither of us knew what it was yet.

I had hope though that I'd be seeing a lot more of his tongue soon.

Aside from the fact our relationship had the budding of something raspberry sweet and chocolate dark, our encounters were friendly. He smiled at me when I laughed or when I flushed—his lips pulling tight around a sharp row of fangs. We gave and took. And I taught myself that he didn't mind my social ineptitude, chatting more than I ever had in my life, since only one of us could comfortably communicate.

Even though Styx was nonverbal for the most part, our conversations were never lacking.

Talking to him was the most fun I'd had in ages, despite it also being the hardest thing I'd ever done. I wasn't good with words. I wasn't good with *friends.* I'd always been a solitary creature but when interacting with someone even more alone than I was, it was surprisingly easy to force myself to open up for him.

He liked Rotho.

I'd been nervous to introduce them at first as memories of his claws sinking inside deer flesh came to mind every time I imagined the encounter. I figured after several nights in his mostly docile company that it wasn't fair to judge him based on our first meeting. So, I very tentatively brought Rotho out, his big, furry body warm where it pressed against my side as we waited together for our nightly visitor. He wasn't afraid. In fact, his tail began to wag as he watched Styx approach. His friendly reaction soothed my very real fears, and I rose to greet Styx without the tension I'd been feeling only minutes earlier.

Styx had cocked his head inquisitively to the side when he saw him, his brow furrowed, a confused, almost constipated look on his face, like he couldn't quite figure out why I'd adopted a creature that was not my own species and turned him into my baby.

"He's my family," I explained. He nodded in acceptance, and then huffed out a put upon sigh. *Strange human*, his eyes seemed to say, though their amber glow flickered with amusement.

I will accept this hairy child as you have.

And now, a week later, with our easy conversation, our camaraderie—and what I could only describe as our courtship behind us—I couldn't wait to see him again. Maybe that made me as odd as people said I was. But if I hadn't cared before, I certainly didn't now.

Life was too short to waste my time worrying about other people's opinions.

I daydreamed about antlers and claws for the rest of the day, anticipation buzzing through my veins. *What would he bring me today?* I couldn't wait to see him. I was learning to appreciate the excitement just as I was learning to appreciate the uncertainty. Any fear I'd felt initially had faded away with the rasp of laughter and the memory of curls dark as burnt cocoa.

When Styx returned that night, he was shy.

Shier than normal.

His eyes were nearly black, hooded by shadow, as he inspected me, his nostrils flaring as he scented the air and seemed to find what he discovered acceptable. I tipped my head back and to the side in a ritual we'd recently discovered, my lashes fluttering as his face dipped down and his lips parted with pleasure in response to my eager submission.

He liked me like this.

Docile.

At his mercy.

His breath puffed along the side of my neck as he scented me, inhaling greedily, a pleased growl rumbling in his chest. I shivered, gooseflesh dancing up my arms as I willed my legs to stay strong, even though I felt about ready to swoon. Styx loved my scent. He sought it out in a predatory, primal sort of way. He liked to skim his nose along my skin, to huff against my shoulders, and scent my wrists and hands—almost like he was trying to figure out what I'd done that day by smell alone. Every time he did it, his cock would perk up where it rested in a bed of wild dark curls, and I'd shudder, weak-kneed as I stared at the flushed red crown. I wished he'd touch me more, but he never did.

I didn't mind the slow burn between us.

I was content to wait.

I liked the way he looked at me.

But most of all, I liked the way he made me feel.

When his eyes were on me, I wasn't the village outcast—the man living in the wrong time. I was just… Ellis, whoever that may be.

And I was *his*.

Yes, the wind murmured, and I made a quiet contemplative noise as Styx stepped forward, closer than before. Out and in, steady, his chest rose and fell with each stuttered breath—almost like he was as eager to see me as I was to see him.

Maybe today we could try something new? A hug perhaps. Or I could invite him inside—I'd take anything at this point. Aside from scenting me we hadn't truly touched, not since that first night when his fingers had shaded my eyes from the distraction of the outside world, and his words had echoed like spring showers inside the back of my mind.

Anticipation burned from the top of my head to the tips of my toes as I waited with bated breath to see what would happen next. Styx touched me, but not in the way I'd been dreaming about, sheets tangled 'round my hips, my toes curled with ecstasy.

He was surprisingly gentle for a creature his size, as his long fingers wrapped around my wrist. My blood sang the moment we touched. Sparks up and down my spine. Despite how gingerly Styx held on, I could still feel the otherworldly strength that exuded from him. He was far stronger than he looked. The longer he held on, the harder it was to ignore the animal inside me that had once screamed to run away from him, as it now begged to run toward him.

It was moments like these, dwarfed by his bulk, and blanketed by his shadow, that reminded me he wasn't human. Styx was *magic*, older than time itself, connected to the earth, the moon, the stars. I had yet to figure out what exactly he was. A monster? A forest spirit? A cursed being, forced to remain inside the forest during the daylight, shackled by his own legend.

There's a monster in the woods.
And if you listen close,
You'll hear its cry,
Echo through the sky,
Its call for blood inside its throat.

Styx tugged me away from my empty tomato plants, his face shrouded in darkness. It was obvious how careful he was not to prick me with his claws or pinch too tight as I followed along obediently, helpless to deny him anything. There was something about the wilderness inside him that called to me.

We echoed each other, like two halves of a whole. Crying out from either end of a cavern through the damp dark of reality.

He was pieced together by magic, and I was a man in search of enchantment.

Our footsteps were quiet in the night-damp dirt as he led me to my barren pumpkin patch, and my brow furrowed in confusion. Styx's other hand still gripped the loaf of bread I'd gifted him that night, gentle as ever, despite the way I knew his talons could sever and maim as easily as they caressed and cradled it.

When we reached the empty patch, confusion hit me like a smack to the face. Because it wasn't empty at all.

There were pumpkins.

Four of them.

They were in their green stage, fat and round, their vines plump and glistening in the starlight. I blinked, scrubbing a hand over my eyes to see if I could clear the hallucination. I hadn't planted pumpkins.

Had I?

No.

No.

I'd been preparing for the following year, not… not this. Had Farmer Jones come over after all? Had he planted them here? *But why?* Pumpkins were his prize-winning crop, the only one he grew that I didn't. He'd been winning with his pumpkins at the Fall Festival for years, always leaping for the sizable reward that accompanied the prestige that came with being chosen as Sacrifice.

There was already so much competition, the idea of him voluntarily planting pumpkins for me was laughable at best.

It didn't make sense.

Why would he do this?

And then… it occurred to me.

Styx made a quiet, grumbly sound beside me and my head whipped toward him as I scanned his face for answers, my heart in my throat.

"*You* planted pumpkins for me," I said softly, voice nothing but honey as my toes curled in the cool dirt and I imagined the way vines might one day sprout from this very spot. I swallowed, my throat tight. "Did you… but—" I shook my head. "But *how?* I mean… they take *months* to grow."

Styx cocked his head at me, like he always did, and I frowned, trying to decipher what he was trying to say as my heart raced and my belly flipped.

"Are they… a gift?" I asked. He'd shown up empty-handed today, that shy expression on his face. *Had this been what he'd wanted to show me? Had this been why he was so nervous?*

He nodded.

Elation buzzed bright inside my chest and I laughed, a soft incredulous sound, unthinkingly swinging an arm around his neck and pulling him in for a tight squeeze. I'd never been a particularly physical person, though I found in most situations when I lacked the words to explain what I was feeling, touch often could answer for me.

Funny how I'd fantasized about hugging him, just a few minutes prior like it was an impossible dream.

He smelled amazing.

He felt even better—strong, sturdy, his skin springy and soft overtop lean muscle. It was hard to reach, admittedly, but I managed, more than a little pleased when he snuffled at my hair, tucking my head beneath his chin.

"Thank you," I breathed, my lips brushing the cool sweat gathering at the base of his throat. Styx made a noise, a helpless little sigh, his fingers tightening around my wrist as he reached around me in an awkward, but eager way—like he didn't know what we were doing right now, but he liked it. He clutched me tightly against his chest and I listened to the way his breath *wooshed* in and out, like a waterfall, or the wind through tall grass.

His heartbeat was erratic.

I wondered at the fact he had a heartbeat at all.

"They're beautiful," I murmured, still breathless. "Thank you."

My hands were buried in the dirt as I watched Styx and Rotho play together. It was a strange sight, though welcome, and I couldn't help but laugh as Rotho tumbled Styx to the ground with a waggle of his big fat butt and the loll of his tongue. Realistically, I knew Styx had to weigh at least 300 pounds; there was no way a dog of Rotho's medium-size could topple him so easily.

Which meant he was *humoring* him.

Styx laughed, the exquisite, rasping sound reverberating through the grass. I wanted that: to join them, to sprint, dance, and race. It took me a moment too long to realize that I could, that I was allowed to. I could do whatever I wanted here with the two of them. Freedom tingled at the tips of my fingers as I rose to my feet, and I chased their bodies with an exuberance I hadn't felt in years. Rotho panted at me, his furry body brushing along mine for only a moment as I bounded with Styx toward my cottage, then the road, the forest, and back to the cottage again.

His smile was ever present, brighter than the moon, wide and sharp. I watched his thighs flex, I watched the swoop of his broad shoulders taper to a trim muscular waist. I watched the way his ass twitched as he launched himself at Rotho only to playfully miss and disappear into the grass.

His antlers still poked up, however, like the fin of a shark, and I laughed, a bright noise that echoed in my chest like the chime of Christmas bells. I felt lighter than I ever had, like if I laughed one more time I'd float away.

Rotho barked and barked and barked, and Styx popped back up, turning to me with twinkling amusement.

Your furry baby is not so bad, his eyes seemed to say.

Dirt clung to my bare feet as I crossed the distance between us. When I launched myself at him, wrapping my arms around the sweat damp heat of his skin, we plummeted to the ground with a happy thump. Styx cushioned my fall, a solid weight beneath me as Rotho wriggled and woofed beside us. The heat of him bled through the thin pair of pajama pants I'd donned to greet him, and I couldn't help but soak him up like a lizard sitting in a patch of sunlight. His long fingers wrapped around my hips, dipping into the crease between my thigh and groin, his expression playful as he squeezed.

A quiet whine left my lips, and his smile grew crooked and mischievous as his nostrils flared and his chest rumbled with a self-satisfied purr.

After he left, I lay in bed, my hand on my cock, those same long fingers flickering in my mind. I pressed my fingers hard into the bruises he'd left behind as I strangled the base of my dick and let my eyes roll back, body melting into oblivion.

Outside my window, the wind whistled again, a voyeur.

This time, I couldn't bring myself to care.

I was too happy.

The next time I saw him, I invited Styx into the house. It was time. At first I'd worried about how he'd fit, but now I knew him well enough to be sure he wouldn't mind how small it was. I wasn't sure what I'd been expecting. Maybe for him to be nervous? Shy? But no. His eyes were bright with interest as he bowed politely through the doorway, forced to crouch so his antlers wouldn't scrape the ceiling. His gaze flickered back and forth as he cataloged the inside of the house, memorizing it, his ever-present curiosity burning bright in his amber eyes.

He sniffed.

Because of course he did.

"I cleaned," I told him, oddly embarrassed, worried that the couch might smell like dirty laundry. I *had* cleaned, but I wasn't sure exactly how strong his nose was. He obviously used it far more than I used mine.

Styx turned to look at me, amusement twitching across his lips.

"Oh, shut up," I laughed and led him to the couch so he could finally sit. He burrowed into it, clearly impressed, his long legs akimbo, the smattering of dark hair across them tantalizing as I imagined the way it might scratch against me if we were to twist together.

He pulled my blanket, the one I'd knitted, over his lap, playing with the soft fibers like he'd never seen anything like it before. He was careful, his claws held gingerly, expression thoughtful. As I watched him, my breath was shallow. Rotho flopped at his feet, uncaring that they were dirty, his tail wagging, brown eyes approving.

It felt strange having Styx inside my personal space.

Not because I didn't want him there or because he didn't fit. But because it had been years since another person had been here with me. I hadn't realized how truly lonely I'd been until he showed me what I'd been missing. I swallowed the lump in my throat as he tipped his head to stare at the photograph of me and Aunt June and Uncle Ruth that hung on the wall.

I'd never had the heart to take it down; though, nowadays, I avoided looking because it only reminded me of what I'd lost. Their place beside me would always remain empty, and I'd made my peace with that. Though sometimes, the loss still felt choking.

In the drowsy moments between sleep and wakefulness, sometimes I'd forget they were gone. I'd forget that I was twenty-seven, that I wasn't a little boy, about to make my way out into the garden to spend the day basking in the sunshine while singing farm songs with my aunt. I'd forget that I'd never have her pumpkin soup again. That I'd never feel Uncle Ruth ruffle my hair. There would be no more birthdays, or Christmases, or laughter.

Who are they? Styx's eyes seemed to ask.

I shook my head, sitting beside him on the couch, my fingers tangling in the quilt close to his. If I reached out my pinky, we'd touch. I wanted to close the distance, but I didn't know how. Suddenly, I felt miles away.

"They're my family," I explained, a tremble in my voice I hadn't realized would be there. "They're gone now. It's just me and Rotho."

Styx nodded, frowning, then he turned to me, his eyes bright and sad.

Inside them, I saw the loneliness I'd always seen inside my own brown eyes. We were the same, him and I. Mirrored pieces of men who didn't know how to love someone new when the gaping holes of those we'd loved before had left us frayed at the edges.

I wanted to kiss him.

I wanted to tell him we weren't alone anymore.

I wanted to say that together we could be a family if he wanted.

Rotho could be his furry baby, too.

But… I didn't say any of those things. I didn't need to. Styx cupped my cheek in one of his massive hands, his claws brushing along my temple as I tipped my head up and our breath mingled.

His pinky tangled with mine.

I wanted him.

I wanted him.

I wanted—

Sitting shiny and young on their vines, the pumpkins Styx had gifted me were growing at an almost alarming rate. Every night when my gentle giant came to visit he helped me tend them, and when there was nothing left to do, we'd turn our efforts to the rest of my garden. We'd pick and pluck, groom and trim, replant and fertilize. He scented me every chance he got, sniffing and huffing happily at my neck like he found me delightful. We didn't need words when our hands were buried in the dirt, side by side. It was intimacy in its purest form. I knew Styx felt it too, the way our roots seemed to reach for each other, desperate to tangle. I could see it in his smile, shark-like and honest, like he didn't realize how very terrifying his teeth could be.

Rotho joined us every night now, and he spent far too much time nipping at Styx's bare heels to get him to play and ignoring me when I called his name to admonish him for bullying our new friend.

We didn't have many of those.

I realized sometime in late August that I had stopped thinking of Styx as a monster at all.

He was just… *Styx.*

Bread lover, animal sympathizer, antlered non-human. Weaver of flower crowns, pumpkin farmer, basket thief. With every new thing I learned about him, the closer we became. There was something special about the connection we shared. It should've frightened me, probably, considering how different we were. The fact I'd never felt this way about someone else should've been a red flag.

Instead he made me feel green, green, green.

Styx made me laugh. He made me smile. He made me want to tell him everything, to spill the deepest darkest parts of me like autumn leaves across the forest floor. And when I was out of words, when I was too tired to speak, and the stars above flickered, the silence we shared never felt heavy.

When he looked at me I became something precious—cherished in a way I hadn't known was possible. Not for someone like me.

All my life I'd told myself I didn't care what people thought of me.

But the truth was, I did.

I just didn't know what to do about it. I didn't *want* to change. I didn't want to be who they wanted me to be. I wanted to exist, peacefully, so I'd pushed away my unease. I'd ignored the comments, I'd laughed at the rumors, I'd eaten every harsh word and joke—ingested them, then tucked them deep inside me, where no one could see how badly they hurt.

Styx didn't want to change me.

He liked me just as I was.

Styx enjoyed everything about me with wide, wonder-filled eyes—like I wasn't an outcast, like I wasn't lacking.

So I baked for him, I laughed with him, I played with him. I gave him everything I'd never given another person. I made him human with every brush of our shoulders, every bump of our thighs, with every shared breath, and every toothy smile. I accepted his gifts, just as he'd claimed, I entered the woods with my heart in my throat—nervous and full of butterflies, and I thought about what it would mean for the both of us, if I became his.

I'd never belonged to anyone but myself.

I didn't know what it meant.

So I shoved the thoughts away and basked in his presence, cloaked by his shadow. I let myself enjoy him, let it be as simple as that. I tucked away every new discovery I made about him into the spot deep inside my chest where I'd kept the harsh words and rumors before. There wasn't room for both, and with every passing day, one of the barbs fell away, replaced instead by Styx's grin.

By the fact he hated tomatoes.

By the fact his antlers felt like velvet.

By the fact he loved my cinnamon bread the most.

I'd discovered this one night when he'd made a point to poke pointedly at the cinnamon loaf where it sat at the end of the line up of presents I'd made for him.

He'd given me a purposeful look. His smile had been soft—so, *so* soft.

This one, his amber eyes said.

This one is the best.

Then he pointed to the garlic and herb loaf and shook his head, and I'd laughed my head off, amused by his antics as he arranged the flavors in the order he liked them. The fact he didn't like garlic made a weird amount of sense. I hadn't connected the dots until he'd explained, but since that first time I'd made him bread, now that he'd gotten more comfortable around me, he wasn't afraid to turn his nose up at it, his face scrunching in disgust.

Maybe it had something to do with the strength of the smell?

Though, when I asked he shook his head at me like he found the fact I cared at all amusing.

Why make anything if it isn't the best one? His face seemed to say.

I couldn't argue with him there.

I liked the cinnamon better, too.

"I can hear you, you know." I tipped my head toward the rustling just off the path, watching the bushes pause their wiggling the moment Styx was caught. It was time to go into town again, unfortunately, but I couldn't bring myself to care the way I used to.

"Styx," I laughed, unable to stop the bubble of happiness from bursting free as I saw him climb out of the bush, clearly embarrassed. I'd noticed that he liked to follow me—like a guard dog, ready to defend me if necessary.

I couldn't help but be charmed.

Especially because the only truly frightening thing in the woods was him.

There were branches caught in his antlers.

When he drew close I rose on the tips of my toes to pluck them away. He looked startled, but he dipped his head, crouching low, so I could reach better when he realized I was trying to groom him.

"You can walk with me," I offered. It was the first time I'd seen him during daylight since our first encounter when he'd been quite literally covered in blood. I'd been so frightened of him then—scared enough I'd tried to pretend he was a figment of my imagination. "You don't have to stalk behind me all sneakily." Styx's cheeks were pink. My belly flipped. "I like your company."

His lips twitched into a pleased little smile as I finished brushing debris from his fuzzy antlers. I pulled my hands back, my heart wobbling all over the place as those amber eyes met mine, glowing hungrily.

My cock stirred, but I ignored it as I tipped my head to the side, exposing my neck like I always did. Styx made a noise, desperate and a little raw as he dove forward, nuzzling behind my ear like a man, starved.

Where should I put my hands? I wasn't sure. *There.* I ended up settling them on his shoulders. His skin was warmer than normal today, almost like his body matched the temperature of the forest. *Huh.* If that was true would it mean that he'd get chillier when winter struck?

"Nnn." The first brush of Styx's nose along my skin always made me quiver. My toes curled, and I let my eyes flutter shut, lids painted red by dappled sunlight. Styx purred in response, satisfied. Tingles shot up my spine as his breath huffed along the shell of my ear. Slowly, inch by inch, Styx traveled down my neck, my chest, my arms, then back to my chest again. He sucked in great big, greedy breaths at my armpits, my belly, and then—

"Oh," I shuddered again, suddenly weak-kneed. His nose pushed against my inseam, a tease that had me spinning. *He probably didn't know what he was doing.* One questioning glance at him told me I was wrong. There was nothing innocent about the way his irises were swallowed black. Or the fact his dick was half-hard, listing greedily to the side, as he buried his face against my balls and dragged in a hungry breath.

I almost burst out laughing when I realized what a sight we made. His massive body crouched over mine as he sniffed, and sniffed, like I was a gourmet meal and not a man dressed in stained overalls with grass in his hair. If someone could see us now—the rumors that would burst like wildfire through town would be ridiculous at best, but not entirely inaccurate.

Ellis Clearwater, the monster lover.

"Styx—" I gently urged his head away, fingers pushing at his antlers. He growled at me. *Growled! What the hell?* I couldn't help but laugh. "Sorry, I'll let you finish then, you greedy thing."

When he was done, he rose to his feet looking very pleased with himself.

His gaze was hot and heavy as he dragged it over my heaving chest and the flush I could feel burning across my cheeks. When he grinned, I nearly lost my balance.

What did the scenting mean?

Instinctually I knew, but I wasn't sure if I was ready to put words to it yet.

"Let's go," I jerked my head south, my blood thrumming as I tried to find my balance again. Sunbeams cascaded through the branches overhead, refracted through Styx's antlers as he held up a finger to stall me, then bounded back into the bushes, all naked flexing muscle.

He returned a moment later with a handful of bright red berries. Gingerly, one by one, he placed them in my palm. I was careful not to move, for fear of pricking myself on his claws, even though I got the feeling he would've rather died than hurt me.

Red juice squeezed from the berries that had bruised, and I popped one into my mouth with a happy hum. Flavor burst along my taste buds as I sucked at the juice, completely at ease, despite not knowing what kind of berry I was eating. Styx would never feed me something poisonous. I got the feeling he knew his way around the woods as well as I knew my way around my garden.

This was his kingdom, like my cottage was mine.

"Thank you," I popped another berry in my mouth, shifted my basket around, and held my hand out expectantly. Styx stared at my face, then my hand, then my face again in confusion, brow furrowed.

His eyes said, *I already gave you all the berries I had.*

"No," I snorted, unable to help myself. "I want to hold your hand." I wagged my hand at him in a way I hoped was enticing and unthreatening. He quirked an eyebrow, looking adorably confused as he hesitantly mirrored me, holding his hand out, palm down, talons glinting. I swallowed the lump in my throat, suddenly embarrassed by how badly I wanted this, as I latched on with my free hand and carefully sandwiched our fingers together.

Styx stared at our hands, his eyes wide with wonder as his cheeks grew pink. We were so *different*, but it didn't matter. I gave him a reassuring squeeze, and in response he released a pleased little rumble that sounded an awful lot like a cat purring. More than a bit smitten, overwhelmed, and happy, I took a steadying breath, and headed down the path.

His hand was warm—massive, honestly. With our palms together, calluses mating, his claws bumping against the back of my hand, our size difference was even more apparent than normal. He towered over me, casting shadow along my body, blocking the sun from view.

Styx continued to stare down at me, still confused, but overall pleased. He gently wagged our conjoined hands, as if to emphasize his question.

His eyes said, *What is this?*

This thing we are doing?

It is nice.

"This is new for me too," I admitted, feeling vulnerable all of a sudden. I popped another berry into my mouth, so as not to waste his gift—and also maybe, to distract myself from the emotions running rampant through my body. Flavor burst citrusy and tart on my tongue, and I sighed, taking a few languorous steps toward town as I let the early autumn air tickle the tip of my nose. "Hand holding, I mean." I blinked, glancing up at him again, embarrassed. "It's for…" God, my cheeks were hot. "It's for—" Styx's free hand gingerly traced the edge of my blush, like he was pointing it out, and I had to force myself not to press a kiss against those gentle, monstrous fingers. My skin buzzed everywhere we touched. "It's for lovers," I confessed. "And friends—" I added quickly, for fear I was acting too forward.

Styx made a questioning sound, then gave my hand a reassuring squeeze of his own. Immediately my racing heart slowed to a gallop, and the tension that had crept into my shoulders bled away.

We held hands the entire way to the edge of the forest.

When I returned, an hour or so later, my basket now full of food, Styx took it from me like a proper gentleman. Balancing the basket on one arm, he held his hand out, palm up this time, and waited. His eyes were warm, expectant.

They were *welcoming*.

I stared at it.

My heart leapt.

It quaked—

It—

I placed my palm in his, and like it was second nature and not something he'd discovered only an hour previously, he slid his fingers between mine and gave the back of my palm a soothing rub with his thumb.

Tree bark scratched at my back, cheerful birds *chirp, chirping* overhead, as I cupped Styx's cheeks in my palms and pulled him down to my height. He'd liked holding hands so much, I'd been desperate to try something new. For days I'd fantasized about doing this with him. The feelings between us were constantly building beneath the surface, like nodes trying to root. I'd been spending more time than I should heading into town lately—as an excuse to see him—though I wasn't sure I was ready to admit that, even to myself.

Night after night, day after day, even when Styx wasn't around he remained beside me in my daydreams.

It was no wonder that I'd broken, the moment I'd seen him today, his eyes full of mischief as he tucked a single white flower behind my ear. I could still feel its petals, tickling my cheek.

What was I supposed to do, *not* kiss him?

Impossible.

"I'm going to show you something," I explained, flushed and embarrassed—and honestly, more than a little terrified. "If you don't like it, that's okay."

Styx crooned softly, chasing my touch like he was starved for it. His eyes blazed with curiosity as he rubbed his cheeks against my palms. *Would he like this? I hoped so. I really, really hoped so.*

My heart wobbled, and I took a steadying breath as I rose onto my toes and closed the last—admittedly small—distance between us. His warm breath caressed my already over sensitized skin, and I couldn't help but shiver, as I built up the courage to do what I'd been dreaming about since that first day we held hands in the woods.

C'mon, Ellis.

I could *do* this.

What was the worst thing that could happen? That he wouldn't like it?

I could deal with that.

When our lips brushed it felt like the world stopped. I could no longer hear the birds. I couldn't feel the autumn breeze. My heart ceased its rabbit-like hops. There was nothing but Styx and his feather-light breath. Nothing but his lips, petal soft. Nothing but the way he trilled quietly, holding perfectly still, like he was terrified of moving, for fear of scaring me off.

When I pulled back, my stomach was full of butterflies. I gasped in a ragged breath, realizing belatedly that I'd forgotten to breathe. My lips tingled. *Did his tingle too?*

I didn't want to look at him, terrified the kiss hadn't made him feel the way it had made me feel.

I shouldn't have worried.

Fingers tangled in the back of my hair, bursting the bubble of my wandering thoughts as Styx tipped my head back and stared at me—*really*, stared. That hungry look on his face was becoming more than familiar. I swallowed, and his gaze snapped to my bobbing throat, before he dragged his attention back to my lips again.

He looked like he wanted to eat me.

Huh.

And then, suddenly without warning, Styx's voice echoed in the back of my mind.

It sounded the same as it had all those weeks ago, throaty and soft, like it was made from the wind itself.

Again, it whispered—*demanded*, really.

Again.

I'd spent so long imagining what his eyes were saying to me, that hearing his voice was honestly startling—relieving too, though. It was clear he wanted this. If I hadn't understood that from the look on his face, the fact he'd actually used words would've clued me in. I got the feeling speaking to me this way was difficult, otherwise he'd do it more often. Which meant… he really, *really* wanted this, didn't it?

He wanted…

Me.

Kissing.

Oh, hell.

"Okay," I breathed, my scalp tingling when he tightened his fingers in my hair, his chest vibrating against mine as he pressed in close and purred. In his own, animal-like way, it almost felt like he was praising me—like that lazy, satisfied rumble was his way of saying, *good boy.*

My lashes fluttered shut, and I pursed my lips, waiting. Styx held me so securely in his grip, I doubted he'd appreciate me trying to break free to close the distance. *No.* He wanted to close it himself.

My theory was proven correct when I felt the huff of his breath against my mouth before his lips met mine and sparks flew again. Styx's kisses were greedy and clumsy at first. I did my best to teach him, through coaxing flutters of our mouths, ebbing and flowing, chasing and retreating.

When he gained confidence, it was like a switch had flipped inside him. Though he remained careful of his teeth, despite his enthusiasm—his mouth was ravenous and demanding. He devoured me, kissing, kissing, *kissing*, like he couldn't get enough of my taste.

My knees threatened to give out, and I was grateful for his grip on my hair and the tree against my back, as I did my best to keep up with him. I had never been kissed so thoroughly or so enthusiastically before. Like not only did he want to feel me, but he wanted to *own* me too. He explored every inch of me, like it was his mission to do so.

When his enthusiasm didn't dim, a foggy sort of peace settled over my mind. I let myself bask in his touch, my tongue lazy and lax as I let him suck and nip until I felt so good, I wasn't sure I was real anymore.

Eventually, I pushed him away. It felt like an eon had passed, but judging by the sun's position above it had barely been an hour. My mouth was swollen and a little numb, in the best way possible, but Styx's was worse. His lips were cherry red, and his eyes were black with desire as he stared at me, his big chest heaving with each stuttered breath.

His cock nudged against my belly, and I shuddered anew.

"I'm gonna guess you like kissing," I said, surprised by how hoarse and quiet my voice was. I didn't think I'd ever sounded like that before.

Styx nodded, his lashes fluttered, a plaintive, begging sort of sound vibrating through his chest into mine. His hard nipples rubbed up against my chest.

More, his eyes begged.

And then he kissed me again.

And again.

And *again*.

The pumpkins were orange now. I stared at them from my window with a fond smile on my face as Rotho lapped at his water bowl in the kitchen and I shoveled the last bite of salad into my mouth. The sun was high in the sky, and I was worn out.

Late nights with Styx were fun, but exhausting. I wasn't used to the change in my schedule, and oftentimes I couldn't fall asleep at all despite how heavy and dry my eyes felt.

It would be easier if I could just live in the woods with him—get used to his schedule. *Was he as tired as I was? Or did he not need to sleep as much as*

I did?

I was startled out of my reverie by a noise out front and Rotho's immediate, angry growl. Sighing, I set my empty plate on the coffee table before I dejectedly stomped my way toward the front door. It was still light out, so I knew my visitor wasn't Styx. He never left the forest during the day, and every time he'd come inside had been through the back door. He probably didn't even know there was another option. Besides, there was only one person Rotho growled at.

My least favorite person in the world.

Oh, goodie.

Farmer Jones raised his hand to knock, but I opened the door before he could touch it. He paused, a little startled, then lowered his hand, his eyes narrowing.

"*Ellis.*" He greeted me as he always did, and I held back my eye roll as I leaned inside the doorway to keep it open. There was no way in hell I was inviting him into my sanctuary, no matter how nice I typically liked to think I was. This space was mine and mine alone. It felt like committing a sin to invite Jones in when just a few nights before I'd had Styx reverently exploring the depths of my home.

"Hiya."

"You told me you hadn't planted pumpkins," he accused, straight to the point. I sighed, unable to help myself this time as I tried to come up with a believable explanation. It wasn't like I could tell him they were *magic* pumpkins and that a forest spirit, or whatever he was, had planted them for me as a gift only a month ago.

Somehow, I doubted that would go over well.

"Looks like I forgot," I shrugged. His beady little eyes somehow miraculously grew more narrow, his face beginning to glow from the force of his angry flush.

"You're not planning on entering into the produce division at the Fall Festival this year, are you?" he asked, an almost pitying twist to his words that I knew was placed there just to make me feel small. Normally, it wouldn't bother me. Normally, the words would roll off my shoulders like droplets of spring rain, but…

These were *Styx's* pumpkins.

A gift.

They were far better than anything growing across the street, no matter how many workers the horrible man hired. And now that he brought it up, like hell was I going to let Farmer Jones win as Sacrifice.

It was the principle of the thing, and I was nothing if not loyal.

"Actually, I am," I told him, even though I had no idea what that would entail—and I'd never planned on doing it—not until he'd tried to intimidate me not to. I'd never been interested in competitions. Never been interested in becoming Sacrifice myself; though, just like everyone who grew up here, I'd seen the red-painted people decorated in ribbons every fall when I'd gone to the festival with my Aunt June and Uncle Ruth.

Farmer Jones's face grew puffier, angrier, his brows lowered, taut with tension, as he grabbed the top of his hat and shoved it down in what was clearly intended as a silent *fuck you*. Rotho growled behind me and I raised an eyebrow at Jones in a way that felt entirely unlike me.

I wasn't a "confront your demons" kind of person.

Well, I *hadn't* been.

Hell, maybe spending time with Styx was doing something to me, evolving me, changing me. I wanted to snap my teeth at him, to growl and posture, to prove that I wasn't scared of surly men with no emotion other than jealousy or anger.

I didn't though. Instead I just *smiled*—beamed, really. "Good day to you, Farmer Jones."

"Well. Good day to you." He grunted at me, a speckle of his spit landing on my cheek. Incensed, he promptly turned and stormed off. He was clearly unhappy with me.

As I wiped the spittle from my cheek and watched him walk away, laughter bubbled up inside me. I stifled it, surprised by my own mirth, until I was safely inside and could giggle like a madman.

Was I insane?

Probably.

I shouldn't have gone around poking the bear with a stick like that. I couldn't bring myself to regret it however, because I knew something Jones did not. He may be a bear of a man, and a brute to match—but I had a brute of my own—and my brute had claws, and antlers, and was more than a little magic.

When I finally calmed down, I crouched to pat Rotho's furry head. He'd stopped growling the moment Farmer Jones was off our property.

"Good boy." I hummed, a giddy feeling lighting me up from the inside out. I chortled my way into the kitchen toward my landline, a fire lit inside my chest.

I had work to do.

Chapter Six

THE HARDEST PART about signing up to participate in the festival was talking to people. When I'd made my way to City Hall, I hadn't been expecting to be bombarded by a million and a half questions. That was my own fault. I should've known it would happen when the woman who ran the Sacrifice every year was none other than Marie Culberry. She'd been my aunt's best friend, though they only spoke to each other on the phone or at their monthly book club.

Marie was… interesting.

Her face moved slower than her words did. Her body buzzed with pent-up energy as she flapped around like a large duck while wearing the world's most festive yellow sundress. Pumpkins, wagons, and all things fall-themed shifted around the skirt as she tapped her lip thoughtfully, and regarded me with barely concealed glee.

For as long as I'd known her, Marie had always worn seasonal prints.

It was something my Aunt June had often laughed about when we'd seen her in passing on trips into town. If Marie could, she'd even match the pattern of her clothing to the book they were discussing that month.

I'd thought she was funny, just like June had.

Now, however, I was anything but amused.

It felt weird to talk to Marie again without Aunt June beside me. Like stepping into the past. I wasn't twenty-seven anymore when I talked to her. I was ten years old, my face hidden in Aunt June's khaki skirt, shy as always.

She was probably the only person in town who had genuinely liked my family. She had quirks of her own, but was widely loved, whereas we'd been outcasts. Despite her own popularity however, Marie had always accepted us as we were. She never minded our outdated lifestyle.

"Signing up this year, are you?" she asked, her words flitting around my ears like moth wings, breathy and high. Blinking away my thoughts, I nodded. Then once again I began trying to catch up as her mouth ran far faster than I could compute.

By the time I finished explaining I was only entering into the pumpkin division, I felt like my head was about to split open.

"It's a good thing, that. No one here's got a green thumb like you do. Can't wait to see the look on Old Jones's face when you beat him." Marie's grin turned wicked, and she let out an evil little cackle before she slid the sign-up paperwork toward me. She clicked her pen once, twice, *three* times before handing it to me.

I stared at it blankly as I processed my feelings.

Maybe it wasn't fair that I was entering with magic pumpkins.

Maybe.

Then again, it wasn't like the world was a fair place anyway. And Styx had given them to me for a reason. I intended to prove to the town that something good could come from the monster they feared so much, even if, at the end of the day, they didn't know it.

So I signed the paper.

And the war began.

Three weeks.

Two weeks.

One week.

One day until the Fall Festival.

Farmer Jones had been projecting hate toward me all month. I could practically feel him glaring at me from across the street, day in and day out, his anger attempting to creep through the cracks into my cottage. He'd take leisurely strolls down the dirt road between our properties just to intimidate me, his beady eyes narrowing in on my thriving pumpkins, spying where they swelled bright orange and plump on their vines.

I'd never seen anything like them, and apparently neither had he.

It was clear from his bewilderment, and the way his naturally ruddy face only grew redder with rage every time he walked away, head shaking. I never caught the words he muttered, and for that I was glad. I was positive I did not want to know the filth spewing from his revolting lips.

Before, his anger would've felt stifling. It would have weighed me down, blanketing me in its cloying, suffocating heat. I wouldn't have been able to think about anything else for hours, maybe days afterward. Caught in a web of his distaste.

I was a different person now, though. I wasn't lonely anymore. I knew now what it felt like to have a friend who appreciated my personal brand of 'different.' Someone who knew me. Someone who understood that even at my prickliest, I was still far more palatable than a sad, angry, man who was so desperate to win he'd harm others to do it.

I pitied him now as much as I'd feared him in the past.

That had been naive.

I should've known a storm was coming, maybe then I could've stopped it.

The day before the Fall Festival I headed into town to gather the ingredients I'd need to bake a rhubarb pie. A celebration was in order. I was officially all signed up, and our pumpkins were primed and perfect. We'd spent hours shining the one that would make it to the fair, and it was quite literally the most beautiful thing I'd ever seen.

Though, if I was being entirely honest, the main reason I'd decided to brave the general population again so soon after my visit to City Hall, was because I craved more feverish kisses, and the brush of Styx's skin against mine. Shaking off those rather tantalizing thoughts, I ducked into the general store with single-minded determination.

Pie.

Styx had never had pie—and he didn't know it yet, but he was about to be mind blown.

Slowly but surely, I'd been introducing Styx to all things baked and sugary, and he'd clearly grown fond of our nightly tradition. Cupcakes had been a win, as had cheesecake. He hadn't known what to think of the lemon bars I made, but ultimately he was a fan.

Pie though?

Yeah, I was ready to change his life.

Excitement buzzed like fireflies in my veins as I took the shortcut through the woods north toward home like I always did, my head held high. Though it was warm still, the autumn wind nipped more harshly than it had since spring, and I inhaled the crisp tickle of it into my throat, my lashes heavy with the red tinge of fading afternoon light.

The wind trailed along the back of my neck and I sighed, tipping my head to the side to give it room to caress. I let my scent twist inside the breeze's searching fingers. It spread between tree trunks, across babbling creeks, and through the overgrown brush toward where my lover lurked somewhere hidden in the shadows.

I listened, and listened, and listened.

If I held my breath, I could tell myself that the snapping of twigs out past the path was just Styx tagging along for the journey, watching over me as he often did from between the barrel of trees as willowy as he was.

He didn't always join me. I figured he must be out hunting for his next meal, or my next present. Maybe he wanted to celebrate tonight as badly as I did. He'd planned this whole thing, after all: the pumpkins, the contest, the Sacrifice. At the end of tomorrow, I'd be his.

I was going to win the Pumpkin Contest.

I could *feel* it.

And when I did, I could sense there was something… *more* waiting in store for me.

The elated feeling bouncing around inside my chest distracted me the entire walk home. I tingled, happier than I'd ever been as I stepped out of the woods and into the tall grass that surrounded the field between the forest and my garden. The ground was squishy from the rainfall from the night before, and I enjoyed the give of it beneath my dirty sneakers as I took a step closer to home. The dry grass brushed against my bare fingertips, autumn blowing its leaves through the golden strands. It tickled, and I almost wanted to laugh—

I was so distracted by my own joy it took me a solid thirty seconds to realize I could hear barking.

Angry, snappish, desperate.

My head snapped up, alarm blazing like wildfire through my body as I dove toward my cottage without thinking. Rotho was *screaming*, his little voice carrying through the screens of my open windows. Why was he screaming? Why was he—

Oh.

Oh.

Oh, God.

Trespassers. Trespassers in my garden. My heart choked its way up my throat as my gaze snapped to the reason he was crying in the first place. Acid threatened to escape as I stumbled, sick.

There were teenagers in my garden.

Six of them.

Their laughter rang in my ears as I watched them raise their farm tools high above their heads before the heavy metal severed the flesh of my perfect pumpkins. It felt like wading through syrup, bile rising as I ran toward them, my head full of cotton. I could hear the *thud, squish* of every impact, though I felt as though I was underwater. This couldn't be real. It *couldn't* be real. Please, don't let it be real.

Thud, squish.

"Stop!" I yelled, my voice strained. *Loud.* I was being loud. I was never loud. I couldn't recall ever raising my voice before. I dropped my basket, and its contents spilled out.

Thud, squish.

I didn't recognize myself.

I didn't recognize the man I'd become as anger flared along my fingertips and I slammed through the gate into my garden. *Thud, squish. Thud, squish.*

"Stop!"

I had to save them.

I had to save them.

The teenagers stopped, their heads raised, their eyes wide. They looked at each other, exchanging alarmed glances. Maybe they hadn't expected me to be home. Maybe they hadn't expected me to confront them at all.

Crazy Ellis.

The freak.

The loner.

The boy who didn't know how to socialize.

Yet, here I was, iron in my belly, my eyes blazing as I stared at them one by one, directly in the eyes, and watched as they shrunk before me. Men becoming small as ants.

Let them be afraid.

Let them realize what they'd done.

What they'd broken.

"We're sorry," one said, a boy smaller than the rest, his voice cracking from the beginnings of puberty. He had pumpkin smudged across his nose, and I tried not to be sick at the thought that it had only minutes prior belonged inside the flesh of the sweetest gift I'd ever been given.

Now that gift lay in ruin at my feet.

All of my pumpkins turned to nothing but viscera.

"*Why would you do this?*" I asked, the bite in my voice wobbling as I realized with a sickening jolt that Styx would come home just a few short hours from now and see how horribly I'd cared for his present. "What have they ever done to you?" My pumpkins, my sweet, sweet pumpkins.

I felt nauseous.

I couldn't breathe—

I couldn't—

Styx would see this. He'd see what a mess I'd made of his gift. He'd be heartbroken. My thoughts spun, and spun, and spun. The world spun, and spun, and spun. Rotho was silent, the kids were too, but all I could hear was the phantom echo of *thud, squish. Thud, squish. Thud, squish.*

The short kid ducked his head. They all did, clearly ashamed. My anger at them melted away as I realized more than likely the children weren't the culprits behind this. Now that I wasn't looking at them without the fog of rage to blind me, I realized they were young. Younger than I'd thought. Wearing the same style overalls I always did, their faces sunburnt from days working out in the fields.

There was only one farmer I knew that hired kids that young.

Only one beady eyed man who would ever do something this vile.

"He said he'd give us double pay," a tall kid spoke up from the back. He had on a lopsided hat and his shovel was clutched tight in his grip, almost like he was afraid I was about to yell at them again.

But I wouldn't.

It wasn't *them* I wanted to yell at.

In a sad way, I could understand why they'd done what they'd done. Most people didn't see me as a person anyway. They had no remorse, no understanding for a boy raised separate from their society.

I swallowed the lump in my throat and shook my head. "Go home," I said softly, the fight inside me, already gone. "I'm sorry for scaring you."

They shook their heads, all six of them, bobbing back and forth from various heights as they gathered their murder-tools and pushed open the squeaking gate to head back to the main road.

I watched them disappear into specks on the horizon and still I stood. Rotho had quieted, though I could sense his worry despite the fact he remained locked safely inside our home. My pumpkins lay in a spray of death at my feet, surrounding me in the perfume of their seeds and flesh.

I tipped my head toward the sky and cried.

Chapter Seven

I CLEANED THE mess the best I could, but there was no disguising what had happened. Rotho joined me and lapped at the smear of salty tears on my face, soothing the worst of my emotion with the leather of his tongue.

His nose was cold and wet where he pushed it against my cheeks and I laughed, ignoring the way he scurried off to chomp his way through pumpkin flesh when he thought I wasn't looking.

I saved what I could.

It took hours to bag it all up and freeze it, and by the time I was finished, the moon had risen high in the sky and there were pumpkin seeds stuck to my skin like glue. Styx would be here soon. He would arrive and he would see what a mess I'd made of his present.

He would leave.

And I wouldn't blame him.

I would lose my family.

I wasn't sure I could survive it a second time.

I didn't have the energy to shower, so instead, I changed into a new shirt that wasn't stained orange with pumpkin guts, then headed outside to wait. The night chill was soothing though shockingly cold as I sat in the middle of my mostly empty pumpkin patch and buried my head in my knees. If I closed my eyes I could pretend none of today had happened. For a moment, things could be perfect again.

All that was left of my pumpkins were the fat green vines that twisted through the soil like serpents decorated in their own lifeblood. I could make-believe all I wanted, but wishful thinking would not bring my pumpkins back to life.

I felt Styx before I saw him.

The wind tickled the back of my neck, the short hairs there dancing as I scrubbed away the wet heat of tears from my eyes and raised my head to meet his gaze. He must've walked over while I was wiping my face because suddenly he was right in front of me. His big yellow eyes glowed, familiar now that I'd gotten the chance to know him better than I'd known another person in all my life.

We shared laughter and companionship without the need for verbal conversation. I'd let him into my garden, my home, my heart.

I swallowed the lump in my throat as Styx sat in the plant debris beside me, his head cocked to the side. He spread his fingers out, gently indicating the vacant vines, though I couldn't see the anger I had been sure would be there—only sadness, curiosity, understanding. There was something haunting about the hollow of his cheeks, the swell of his slightly too full lower lip, the cast of shadows across his cheekbones from his swathe of soil-dark curls. He was as enchanting now as he'd been the first day we'd met. This time I was frightened for an entirely new reason.

Terrified he'd leave me.

"They broke them," I explained, my voice wobbling as the words escaped like broken shards of glass. "Jones… he… he told them to do it."

Styx's eyes darkened, his expression hardening as he nodded. A beat passed as he seemed to debate with himself before he reached out with gentle hands, and enveloped my wrists in his grip. I sagged, grateful he still wanted to touch me after everything that had happened.

"Styx—" His name was a prayer for forgiveness.

Before I could begin to plead, he silenced me. His body was soothing and solid against mine, as he pulled me in close, curled his arms tight around me, and helped me hold my broken heart together. I wasn't sure why I was so surprised that he was hugging me. Despite the speech barrier, we'd never lacked intimacy.

But I was.

Surprised.

How long had it been since someone comforted me when I was sad like this? How long had I carried my burdens in silence?

My head cushioned on his bare chest, my cheeks sticking to him with sweat and tears and the leftovers of my own heartache. As I listened to the stuttery *thud, thud* of his heartbeat I finally began to relax. I hadn't been held like this in so long, I had forgotten what it felt like. I'd forgotten the way my lungs learned to expand again, the breath rushing in, in, in. I'd forgotten how much easier it was to bear the world's weight while wrapped in arms stronger than my own. My hands quivered as I wrapped my arms around his firm body. Styx clutched me impossibly close, awkward, sweet, and entirely inhuman despite this small piece of humanity. He inhaled with a soft sigh, his breath tickling my skin as he scented my sadness.

"I'm sorry," I hiccuped against the hollow of his throat. Styx growled softly in admonishment, as if to say, *it is not your fault.* Nuzzling his nose into my curls he greedily breathed me in. He made me feel like I had become a summer breeze, or a spring rain. Something worthy of such worship could only come from nature itself.

I didn't want to leave his embrace.

But I needed to know what he was thinking.

When I pulled back, Styx had forgiveness written on his face. *Thank God, he wasn't angry.* Relief bubbled and burst forth as I launched myself at his lips with an enthusiasm I had never felt for another person before.

Monster or not, he was mine, just as I was his.

Today his lips tasted like creek water and something musky and masculine with an undercurrent that was almost sweet, like fresh raspberries straight off the bush. They were soft. Softer than sunflower petals, softer than spools of fresh yarn, softer than the velvety skin on the outside of peaches hiding the even more tender flesh within.

Styx made a noise, a happy growly sort of sound.

It was confused.

It was hopeful.

It was *wild.*

He kissed me back, and the world was right again.

He kissed me back, and I knew we were fine.

Styx's kisses were as enthusiastic as they were unpracticed. He was better than he'd been when we started, but his excitement sometimes got in the way of technique. His tongue was hot as it played with the seam of my lips, slipping inside with no timidity. He licked along the roof of my mouth, and I whined, toes curling in the dirt. I choked on my desire for him at the same time I choked around his tongue.

"Nnng," I shuddered, letting him play with me how he liked—allowing him to eat me just like I'd feared he would the day I'd met him, blood-covered, in the forest. Spots swam in my vision as he devoured me, greedy kiss by greedy kiss.

When it came time to breathe, I had to force him away. My fingers held onto his surprisingly smooth cheeks so he wouldn't go too far, as I stuttered in a breath of crisp fall air, and giddiness made my head spin. It was hard to believe how desolate I'd felt only minutes before. Hard to believe that someone could make me so happy, I could forget something as traumatic as what had just occurred.

Styx was magic, in more ways than one. He made me lightheaded and happy. Though, there was no avoiding the emotional whiplash that came as a result of quickly flipping from heartbroken to elated.

The last ten minutes felt like a dream.

I couldn't believe how thoroughly I'd just been kissed.

Tongue-fucked, more accurately.

Styx grinned at me, this *feral* bright thing, his eyes radiating happiness as he lunged forward and I squeezed his cheeks to keep him from moving. Laughter burst free at the pouty look on his face. I didn't blame him. I wanted more kisses, as much as he apparently did.

"Thank you," I hummed, my cheeks hurting from the force of my smile.

He nodded.

Then his face shuttered, darkness passing over him as he reached over to push a wayward curl behind my ear. I shut my eyes and his voice whispered in the back of my mind. It was the third time I'd heard it, but it never became less special.

I will fix this, he promised.

His talons scraped soothingly against my scalp, and I shuddered, holding still as my eyes fluttered open once again and I watched the moon flicker between Styx's antlers. He held me like something precious. His eyes were worshipful, like a man at an altar.

No one had ever looked at me like that, until him.

"How?" I asked softly. "They're already gone."

He looked around at the empty pumpkin patch, a thoughtful frown on his face, the shadows a slash across his hooded eyes. With a calculating twist to his lips, he cataloged our surroundings before he turned back to me, his eyes dark with something that looked like revenge.

Fear flickered in the pit of my stomach, but excitement did, too.

Revenge, his eyes said.

I will avenge you.

Farmer Jones's pumpkin patch was barren of people this late at night. I followed after Styx as he scented the air, his nose held high, then low, then forward as he strode through grass and dirt with purpose to his destination.

He was a man with a plan.

Yet, I had no idea what the plan was.

I asked him, but he didn't answer. His eyes were blazing as he glided toward the tall wooden fence that separated the greenhouse from the rest of the property. I wondered distantly if he was scenting the pumpkins in the air. Farmer Jones always stored them there after he'd cut them from their vines. He'd sell them at the fair, then at the front of his farm as guests lined up to visit his corn maze.

In a row along the fence were various signs, despite the fact the festival hadn't happened yet.

"This Year's Sacrificial Pumpkins!"

"Come Get Award Winning Pumpkins Here!"

"Jones The Magician Does It Again!"

What a dick.

As I admired the way Styx effortlessly leaped over the fence as gracefully as an antelope, the tightness in my chest broke free. All this time, I'd been trying to reconcile the man with the beast in front of me, but I realized in a moment of clarity what Styx truly was.

Both.

Neither.

It didn't matter.

He was a cool breeze. He was the rush of rapids. He was the dry heat of summer. He was the crunch of autumn leaves underfoot. He was comfort. He was hungry kisses. He was two pinkies tangling to show solidarity, when the loneliness crept in.

He was *Styx*.

Monster, man, friend, and mate.

He was home.

I climbed over the fence after him, though my descent was far less graceful. Despite my long legs, I couldn't leap the way he did, and I ended up twisting my ankle a little as I stumbled along after him, wobbly as a newborn calf.

When we reached the door to the greenhouse, my heart was in my throat. What was he up to? I had no idea what was about to happen; though, I could only imagine what Styx, a creature who seemed to be ancient, would think was a fair trade for what had been taken from me.

I wouldn't be his Sacrifice this year.

I couldn't be given to Styx, the way both of us wanted.

Even still, I felt conflicted about seeking revenge. As much as I hated Jones, I refused to hurt his produce or pumpkins. Though, when I thought about it, I seriously doubted Styx would ever do something that abhorrent. Plants were sacred. We both agreed about that.

The door was locked, and for a moment I was struck with relief.

Maybe we wouldn't go inside after all?

Wrong.

The door clicked open, and I blinked in surprise as Styx whipped around to give me a smile that was all jagged pearly white teeth.

So, he could unlock doors.

With magic, apparently.

Okay.

I suppose that wasn't as weird as the fact he could summon magic pumpkins or speak to me inside my head. All things considered, lockpicking seemed to be the least 'fantastic' of his powers.

I couldn't believe, sometimes, how absolutely amazing Styx truly was. For so long, I had wondered why he had chosen me of all people. Though, the more time we spent together, the more I was beginning to understand. We fit in a way that shouldn't have worked, but it did.

I was so glad that he was really here and not a figment of my lonely imagination. Some part of me hadn't yet realized that he could interact with the real world just as easily as he lived inside the sanctuary of my garden. If I had, I would've been even more grateful that he'd chosen me. That he was here, avenging me, because he cared.

The lights inside the greenhouse were switched off and the plants rested, shadowy figures of rounded giants laid out upon hay as pale as weak summer sunlight. I swallowed, anticipation buzzing just beneath the surface of my skin as Styx wandered into the darkness.

What was he going to do?

The more I thought about it, the more I realized I didn't care.

I was just happy to follow him, my attention caught by his back muscles while they tensed and flickered—enraptured by the way his lean but powerful thighs pulsed with strength. He examined every nook and cranny of the greenhouse with a determination I didn't understand, his big body far more tempting than it should've been.

The anxiety that had been simmering inside me came to a boil as I glanced through the foggy white walls, trying to see if the farmhouse lights had been turned on. If I could see the house, chances were anyone inside it would be able to see us.

I didn't know what we were doing here, but I sure as hell didn't want to get caught doing it.

My fingers twitched at my sides, brushing along the scratchy fabric of my overalls, seeking familiarity as my hands grew clammy with nervous sweat.

What would happen if Farmer Jones found us here?

What would he do?

When I glanced back at Styx, he had an arm full of blankets. My forehead wrinkled in confusion as I watched him lay them out in the middle of the open walkway between rows of fat orange pumpkins. His eyebrows were furrowed in concentration. A swathe of dark curls obscured most of his face as his powerful arms flexed, veins flickering, and my mouth grew dry.

Just minutes ago, I'd been wrapped tight in those arms. I'd had his tongue inside my mouth. I squirmed, just remembering. But then confusion overpowered my lust again and I cocked my head to the side in a mirror of the motion Styx always made, as I tried to figure out what he was doing. Building… something? Dust powdered up as he arranged his blankets, piling them, bunching them, folding them until they resembled a giant nest.

Ah.

Did he want to… to *sleep* here?

Why?

Where had he gotten blankets in the first place?

That question was answered for me rather quickly when I glanced around again and realized he'd gathered the items from a long line of shelves at the back of the greenhouse. I hadn't noticed them initially upon entry, but Styx apparently had. He bounded back to the shelves, gathered the last of the blankets, and returned, ignoring me for several impossibly long minutes as he continued to stack and pile them all together.

Confused, anxious, and fascinated, I couldn't tear my eyes away.

Eventually, Styx stopped moving. He shifted back on his heels, crouching with his thigh muscles tensed. I stared at the swathe of dark curls at the base of his dick, distracted, while he admired his work, finally deciding his nest was complete.

For what, I didn't know.

It *did* look comfy, though.

Styx rose to his full height effortlessly, gracefully. His antlers brushed along the top of the building as he took a step closer, all long legs and thick cock, the hair on his chest stark in contrast to the pale moonlight that decorated his skin. I wanted to lick it. I wanted to lick *him*.

I closed my eyes.

Patience, I urged myself. *He's only just learned about French-kissing.*

I shouldn't have worried.

Come, the wind whispered.

I went.

Styx pulled me to his nest by the wrist, always careful, always aware of how easily his claws could separate my flesh from my bones. Our first encounter had been painted in blood and viscera, but somehow I couldn't find it inside myself to be afraid.

If he wanted to eat me, I would have let him.

Luckily his desires were far less macabre.

Styx guided me to lay in the pile of blankets, gentle, as if he was handling something priceless. They were soft against my back. I couldn't feel the hard floor beneath them as I stared up at him, confused but excited. *This was new.* We'd never been horizontal together before. My heart was in my throat as I spoke, voice nothing but a quiet croak.

"Is *this* your revenge?"

Styx shook his head, then pursed his lips in thought. After a moment, he changed his mind and nodded, a playful twist to his features. Yes and no. Unclear.

I laughed when he did. Rough and barking, the sound vibrated the space between us. His mouth split wide into a big, sunny smile. The innocence of our laughter was at odds with the rough way he shoved my legs apart with greedy fingers, and nestled down in the V between my thighs. My cock twitched. I'd been half-hard since I'd walked behind Styx across the field and had ample time to admire the curve of his meaty ass.

Styx made a pleased sort of noise, rubbing his hips from side to side, like he was trying to feel my dick through the fabric. There was a sticky spot forming on my overalls where precum collected. I could feel the slick, slip-slide of it as he teased me and my breath left my body in a punched out *woosh*. I shuddered, unable to help the way my hips jerked up to meet his, as my knees went weak, and I watched Styx's smile fade away.

The playfulness was gone.

In its place was hunger.

His nostrils flared.

His eyes flooded black.

I only had a second to mentally prepare before my world turned dark as he enveloped me, his tongue slipping so far inside my throat it was a wonder I could breathe. Choking, and twitching, I let my eyes roll back and all my inhibitions fell away. Kissing. *I loved kissing.* Sweet bliss overwhelmed my senses as I sucked and licked back, giving back as good as I got, my head full of bees as I scratched along Styx's chest, searching for something to hold onto.

I could hardly breathe, and I'd never been happier.

Styx was ravenous. His massive hands were hot and leathery as he slid them from my wrists, up my arms, then across my shoulders and down my sides. The only reason I even realized he'd divested me of my clothing with a flick of his dexterous claws, was because of the chill that hit my skin the moment the tearing sound that filled the air stopped.

I wanted to be mad that he'd ruined my favorite pair of overalls, especially when I realized I'd be walking home naked now, but I couldn't bring myself to care.

Styx was heat, wilderness, and wanton abandon.

His nails pricked me, and the bite of pain only made me moan, my head spinning, lungs crying for oxygen. He was so big, so fucking big—crowding me into the dirt, possessive and demanding. When it felt like I was about to pass out and I couldn't handle the lack of air any longer, I pushed weakly at his chest, and he pulled back immediately.

He didn't move far.

Blinking my eyes open, my vision was foggy with lust-induced tears. Sticky wet lashes brushed my cheeks as I shuddered out a broken, desperate breath that sounded suspiciously like a sob.

"Please," I murmured, though I didn't know what I was asking for. Only that I wanted more—that I wanted *him*, whatever he would give me.

Sex had never felt like this.

Like my body, my heart, my mind were all connected.

Styx made a noise, deeper than the rumble of a thunderstorm. I exhaled another ragged breath and watched the way his amber eyes glowed beneath the fall of his raven-colored bangs.

Be wary of yellow eyes.

The poem I'd memorized in my childhood came to mind again as I reached up with trembling fingers and traced along the swell of his prominent cheekbone. He'd touched me like this many times. It felt almost poetic to mirror the gesture, especially now, with our bodies closer than they'd ever been before. I tucked his hair behind his ears, watching him through my wet lashes as his nostrils flared and he began to purr.

There's a monster in the woods.
And if you listen close,
You'll hear its cry,
Echo through the sky,
Its call for blood inside its throat.

Those words had always felt like an omen. I now knew, however, that the cry the poem claimed to be a call for blood was anything but that. It was loneliness. A bid for companionship, for camaraderie, for understanding. The monster everyone was so afraid of had long since evolved from the monster that poems had been written about, into the creature I saw before me now.

Mate, the wind whispered.

Mate.

I should've been frightened.

I should've run.

I should've done a lot of things.

I did exactly none of them as I pulled Styx's head down by my grip on his cheeks and licked along the seam of his lips with purpose. His entire body shuddered. His hips jumped against mine.

"If you want me," I told him, a promise drifting through moonlight and dust, the scent of pumpkin in the air, "I'm yours."

I pictured springs in our garden, summers in the woods. I pictured autumn leaves in fall and Rotho's panting as he looped between our legs. I pictured winter snow and antlers warmed by knitted blankets. I pictured warm bread and clawed fingers gently severing the loaves piece by piece.

I wanted forever, whatever that might be.

Maybe my forever wouldn't be as long as his would, but it was the best I could give, and it was enough.

Styx's next kiss meant, *thank you.*

It meant, *I love you.*

It meant, *mine.*

His tongue was wet and iron-hot as it dragged over my collarbone. I whimpered. He was careful of his teeth like always as shivers danced up my spine and gooseflesh flickered across my arms. My nipples pebbled in the cold and Styx's tongue swirled around them, curious.

When I gasped, he did it again.

And again, and again, and *again.*

My cock jerked, red and swollen with need, weeping eagerly against my stomach. Precum glistened in the moonlight where it marred my freckled skin and wet the thatch of nearly auburn curls that danced from my dick up my belly. I had never been this hard before, this desperate. *How many times had I dreamed of this? Of touching him?* Of that tongue—all over my body.

I couldn't stop shaking, my need was so great. And with each breath I took, Styx's expression only grew more smug. He liked what he was doing to me. The way he was taking me apart, piece by piece, lick by lick. Hot and slippery, his tongue twisted and pulled at my nipple and I *whined,* my head falling back against our nest of stolen blankets, as his amusement buzzed through the air.

He gave the other nipple the same teasing attention. They stood up, red and flushed, glistening with his slippery, lube-like spit. Obscene. My belly jumped, my dick leaking as I stared down my chest at the mess he'd made of my body.

I needed more.

God, please.

I needed it.

"I thought you were supposed to be a beast," I reminded him, my toes curling as I shoved my heels into the back of his thighs, pulling him closer against me. Our hips met and his cock ground against mine. My clothes lay in tattered pieces at my sides, but I ignored them, as I licked my lips and stared. The fat, engorged tip of his cock pushed through his foreskin. His dick was as greedy as the rest of him, darker red than mine was, precum dripping as the vein on the underside throbbed. He wanted this as badly as I did, he just needed a little push. "I've had humans that were more ready to fuck."

Styx growled, a primal, furious noise. His eyes flashed with possessiveness as his gaze met mine and his lip curled. A drop of precum hit my abs, and I trembled as his pleasure marked my body, and the flash of Styx's vicious white teeth flickered in the low-light.

He didn't like the thought that someone else had fucked me. My dick jerked, more than a little on board with his current mood change. Maybe I shouldn't tease him, but it felt deserved. He'd been teasing me, after all.

Besides, I found his possessiveness kinda cute—like a dog with his favorite toy. I didn't mind being owned if it meant getting that fat, thick cock inside me. It was larger than my own, in every way. Thick, long, wider at the base than the top. I had never wanted to have someone rearrange my insides the way I wanted Styx to.

How was it possible to want someone this much?

Despite how desperately I needed him to own me, I couldn't help but laugh. Those razor sharp teeth didn't frighten me. His eyes flashed with amusement as I shoved playfully at his head with enthusiasm. He barely moved, but it was obvious he appreciated the game. I could see the twinkle in his eyes as he grinned at me, long, slippery tongue dripping as he panted.

"I want you. Isn't that enough?"

Gone was the possessive beast, once again. Instead, he was playful. *Mean.* He ignored my complaints as he continued to tease me. His tongue slid between my pecs, traced my Adam's apple, then climbed back down to torture my already abused nipples again. By the time he finished the second time, they were swollen and raw. In the frigid night air, they glistened with the remnants of his saliva. Every time the wind tickled across them I couldn't help but whimper, jumping away from the overstimulation. *Fuck.* The way he looked at me made my blood sing.

Styx leaned back, self-satisfied, his lips pulling into a smug grin.

I'd been seeing a lot of that smug grin tonight.

I couldn't say I minded.

Then, like a switch had been flipped as Styx admired his work, something flickered in his eyes, dark and animalistic. The look he gave me was primal in a way I had only ever glimpsed from him before. He was always careful around me. He kept his animal side in check.

Now though?

The man between my legs was all predator.

I shuddered.

Styx observed me hungrily. He watched the way my pupils dilated, watched the way my breath stuttered in my throat, my fight-or-flight instincts automatically kicking in the moment they registered the presence of a true predator.

His antlers were a crown atop his head, the king of the woods, a prince among mortals.

He was monstrous and beautiful, cruel as only nature could be.

My breath rushed from my lungs as Styx grabbed my hips, his nails pricking into the soft skin as he abandoned torturing me, and began dragging his nose and tongue down my sternum with purpose. It tickled a little, and I gasped, my lashes fluttering as I stared at him with my lips parted in fascination. There was no word to describe what he was doing to me, this desperate little snuffle-grunt as he inhaled the scent of sweat on my skin and his tongue lapped at the saltiness.

Down, down, down he went.

By the time he reached my cock, I was whimpering. My head tossed back, fingers tangled in the soft hair between his antlers.

"Fuck—"

Styx snarled, his nose buried in the nest of curls at the base of my dick. I twitched and his growl grew in volume, his cat-like eyes luminous as he glared at me as if to say *hold still*. I did my best to comply, though the way he scented and tasted the fragile skin around my balls had me whimpering and writhing. It felt so amazing I could hardly get a breath in.

I spread my legs to give him more room, trying not to be incredibly overwhelmed by how good it felt to be touched. He was thorough, desperate, and ravenous. Styx sucked kisses into my inner thighs, and scraped his teeth along the tendons. By the time his tongue wrapped around my cock, tears were leaking across my cheeks. Never had sex been so overwhelming, so… intimate.

It had always been a means to an end before.

Now it was heaven.

It was sex the way it was supposed to be. Not scratching an itch, but an experience between lovers, a communion of souls. His heart and mine, beating the same rhythm.

Too soon, he released my dick, and I sobbed.

"No, no, no, no—" My hips jumped and he rumbled a warning. I froze, terrified I'd scared him off. Luckily, that wasn't the case. He didn't stop touching me. Thank God. Moving into uncharted territory, his curious tongue slid behind my balls. The skin there was more sensitive than everywhere else, and the rigid stroke of his tongue had my eyes rolling back as I cried out, shocked and excited.

No one had ever licked me there where I wanted it the most. I spread my hips wider to give him more room to work as I reached down to pull my knees apart, exposing my already aching entrance to him. Styx made another grunty-growl noise, pleased as it vibrated against my sensitive flesh and he stroked his tongue, inch by inch, along my taint. My hole twitched, begging for something—anything.

"Styx," I gasped, my head tossed back against the blankets, my cock leaking a steady drip onto my abs as I released one knee so I could touch myself. Before my fingers could meet the feverish skin Styx slapped my hand away, gentle but firm. "Please!" I was begging. I'd *never* begged, especially in bed. *What was happening to me?*

Styx brought something out in me that I knew had always been there—hidden behind the surface of my person-suit. I felt like I was looking into the mirror for the first time. Seeing myself, for who I could be—who I should've been, all along.

It was raw, it was real, it was authentic.

All thoughts left my head as he began licking in earnest, my free hand slipping in the sweaty crease behind my knee again as I spread myself as wide as I could. Pleasure buzzed from the top of my head to the tips of my toes and my mouth grew dry as I whined like a hurt animal into the brisk night air.

Just a little lower.

I just needed him a little lower—

When Styx's tongue slipped deeper into my crease, I gasped.

He was so close to where I wanted him—*so close*.

The muscle was dexterous and warm, slicked with a substance that was closer to lube than spit. I could still feel the way it clung to my skin, making my nipples shine in the waning moonlight where it diffused through the white walls.

What if he didn't know what to do?

What if he didn't plan on fucking me?

My thoughts spun.

Styx's tongue flickered over the sensitive skin at my crease and I keened, loud and broken, uncaring of the farmhouse only fifty yards away. I had been so terrified of being seen earlier, it was almost poetic how little I cared now. My legs trembled from the strain of holding myself open, my hole twitching and trembling as I waited with bated breath for him to bury himself deep in the one place I wanted him most.

"Please," I begged softly, unable to recognize my own voice. "I need it." My breath left in a broken burst. "I need you."

Styx made a curious sounding noise, his dark head bobbing as he glanced up at me one last time, a desperate heat in his eyes like he just couldn't help himself. His attention shifted to my hole where it twitched with need, and his eyes fluttered shut as he let out an overwhelmed, starved little noise. He wanted inside me as much as I needed him there.

Thank God.

Oh—

The first time his tongue flickered along the sensitive skin of my hole, I sobbed. He did it again, and I clenched around nothing, aching for more as he played with me, licking, licking, licking, until I relaxed enough that he could slip his way in.

The way he wriggled inside me was far more dexterous than a human tongue would be able to be. The feeling was different, probably. He was longer, thicker, able to curl and rub more efficiently with the help of his slippery spit.

I hiccuped, shuddering through the sensation as he forced his way deeper, deeper, and deeper still. He didn't let me adjust to the intrusion, he didn't pause. I could feel—and hear—this possessive growling noise building up inside his chest, as his tongue grew thicker the further he pressed inside me. He was tasting me, devouring me. Fuck, he was thick. My eyes rolled back and my hole squeezed desperately around him, trying instinctually to fight off the greedy beast.

I wanted his cock in my mouth.

I wanted his tongue to choke me.

I wanted him to fuck me till my eyes crossed, my head was empty, and my ass was raw.

After what felt like eons, Styx finally decided it was time for a change of scenery. I only had a moment to adjust to the emptiness as he pulled his tongue out of my ass, grabbed my hips with purpose and flipped me over. The breath *wooshed* from my lungs as my face smashed into the soil-scented blankets. *What?*

Styx's hands were demanding as he shoved my legs beneath me, adjusting my body until my knees nestled in the blankets and my hole was exposed, slippery and gaping to the brisk night air. With a dominating grip on my hips, he tucked his thumbs into my crease and forced my cheeks open wide. *Fuuuck, it felt good.* My head spun as he kneaded at my ass, testing its jiggle with a happy little grunt. My skin stung from his claws, as I trembled in anticipation. The emptiness was the worst part. I wanted him inside me again, more than I wanted to take my next breath.

I would gladly suffocate inside the blankets if it meant feeling him stretch me open on the thick, wet width of his cock.

Without warning, pain lanced through my body. I cried out as Styx sunk his teeth into the meat of my ass, marking me as his. The sting was short-lived, luckily, as I was immediately distracted by the swipe of his tongue, soothing the marred flesh. He lapped at my blood with a helpless whine, like he couldn't help the way he wanted to taste me, all of me, every last drop—but he felt sorry he'd had to hurt me to do so.

"Fuck me," I pleaded, my voice broken as dry fall leaves. "Fuck me, fuck me, fuck me."

Styx didn't fuck me.

The bastard.

Instead, his tongue slipped back along the crease between my cheeks, wet-hot as it traced over my gaping hole again. I sobbed, desperate and broken, shoving my hips back against his face. So full, so thick—but not enough—not what I wanted.

"*Fuck-me-fuck-me-fuck-me*," I chanted, desperate and loud, my head swimming. My clothing lay in tatters around me, buried in our nest like it belonged there. There was no need for humanity here, not with him, not now.

Styx's tongue slipped further in, far deeper than he'd been able to go before due to the new angle. I howled as he licked along my inner walls, feeling around like he was searching for something.

"Lower," I gasped, muffled by the blankets. My dick ached as it dragged against my belly. "Just a little… lower." I drew in a ragged breath, reaching for my cock again, despite the strain in my shoulders. I stopped halfway there when I remembered the way he'd slapped me away earlier. *If I disobeyed him now… would he stop?* It wasn't worth the risk. I dropped my hand. All the while, Styx's tongue searched, thorough, hot and slick as he spread me wide and my body stretched to accommodate him.

When he found what he wanted, electricity shocked my whole body as his tongue pressed with purpose against my prostate.

"There!" A noise escaped me I'd never made before. My ass tightened around him.

Styx growled in triumph.

He rubbed, flicked, and sucked at my sensitive rim until I could do nothing but sob and gasp, his tongue toying with the spot inside me that had me seeing stars. My body opened beneath the torrent of his attention like a flower opening its petals toward the morning light. With every languid thrust of his tongue I became looser, softer.

When Styx pulled out again I couldn't help the way I babbled and cried. The blankets beneath my face were wet with my tears as my body ached to be filled again. I wasn't even sure what words I was saying, only that my desperation must've finally been enough, because I could feel him shuffling behind me, his muscular thighs pressed tight to mine. He snarled, a dangerous, sexy sort of noise, as he snapped his teeth at the back of my neck, sharp and threatening.

Stay down, bitch, they said.

Stay still.

Obedient.

I groaned my assent, too exhausted by my own pleasure to do anything but shuffle my ass toward the swell of his cock, my face buried in stolen blankets. My hole was sloppy and wet, trembling, as it did its best to close, but it had been too thoroughly stretched to do so. The scent of fall was embedded in the fabric, pumpkin sap stuck along my cheekbones as I tilted my hips back, searching for him.

Submitting to Styx felt like second nature.

It was how it should be. Me, with my ass up, ready to be fucked.

The thick head of Styx's dick brushed against my ass cheeks, and I whined as I felt the sticky drops of his precum decorate my skin. He dragged it along my crease, across the swell of my ass, pressed his crown into my dimples, and my inner thighs, until his precum had marked every inch.

My rim sucked eagerly at his crown when he finally, finally pushed against my needy hole. Big. *So, big.* Even stretched as I was, when he pressed in I couldn't help but cry out. He was thick. Thicker than his tongue had been. I couldn't wait to feel every inch of him. I don't know why, but I assumed that he'd work his way inside as slowly as he had prepped me. I was prepared for it to be pleasured-torture, inch by inch, just as everything else until this point had been.

I was wrong.

He was an animal. Styx fucked forward, a beast on a mission—anything to get his dick inside me. All his humanity had floated away like cotton in the wind as he buried his face against the back of my neck, and he snapped his hips hard against my ass. Every inch of that glorious, monster cock slid in with a quiet pop. "Uh," I panted, unable to do anything but take it, as he pulled out, and slammed back inside again. My cheeks bounced, rippling as he fucked back and forth, all finesse abandoned, as he hissed through his teeth and took what he wanted.

Being used by Styx was a religious experience.

I let him have me, just as I'd promised, face down, ass up.

He split me wide, seeking his pleasure, and I moaned, uncaring of who might hear, uncaring of the mess I was making of the blankets beneath me. The only thing that mattered in that moment was how my body opened for the thick swell of Styx's dick.

He didn't stop me this time as I reached down to touch myself. My fingers wrapped around my crown and I dug my thumb into the slit at the top, sticky and sweet, my own cum coating my fingers as my hips jolted with each of Styx's eager thrusts.

I grasped my cock, dragging my hand from root to tip, pleasure so intense it made my brain short-circuit, buzzing like a live wire through my body. He fucked me with little to no grace, though somehow managed to hit my prostate dead on with every snap of his hips. There was something about the earnest, desperate way he took me that only made the experience more intoxicating.

When I came it was with a loud, broken wail, the sound so unlike me, yet so instinctual I knew it came from the part of me that lay buried beneath the human-suit I'd donned from birth. The beast within me was desperate for its time in the light.

Trembling, on my knees, I let him use me.

Now that I'd found my pleasure, Styx only fucked me harder. The steady slap-slap of his hips slamming into my ass was loud and wet, the slippery glide of his unnaturally slick spit keeping me open and receptive as he buried his teeth in my shoulder. *Fuck*. Pain burst from the bite and I hiccuped, my words spilling like a waterfall between us.

"Take me, take me, take me," I begged, my hole clutching tight around him as his chest rumbled, and he picked up speed for one last burst of rapid-fire thrusts, before he finally spilled hot and wet, deep inside my body.

I had never felt so thoroughly claimed in all my life.

All the parts of me that had felt wrong, shifted into place. Styx's large body crowded over mine, his cum leaking from my still twitchy, loose hole. And as he sucked and licked at the bite on the back of my neck, I came to terms with the fact I had never been happier.

We lay gasping into the blankets for a long time.

Too long.

When I lifted my head, it was to see a familiar pair of sturdy yellow work boots standing in the doorway.

Laughter burst free from my chest as I dragged my gaze up Farmer Jones's pajama-clad legs to the horror written across his ruddy pug-like face.

"What the actual hell—" he started, only to be cut off when Styx's tongue left my neck and he slowly, so slowly, lifted his head to meet the other man's gaze. A chill ran down my spine. Styx's bulk crowded over me, his body a protective shield as the acrid scent of fear filled the air.

His growl echoed ominously through the silence—a warning, a threat, a promise all at once.

It said, *leave.*

It said, *he's mine.*

It said, *I'll kill you.*

Affection bubbled up my throat and turned into another laugh. I couldn't bring myself to care about the ridiculousness of the situation we were in, as Farmer Jones turned around and ran. He was out the door quicker than I could blink, his striped pajamas disappearing back up the hill toward his house.

He wasn't a very fast runner, so I got to enjoy his escape, cackling a little when he tripped on the porch steps and nearly lost a shoe in the mud. Served him right, for all the years he'd terrorized my family.

I wasn't the kind of person that wanted to hurt others.

Scandalize them, though?

That, I didn't mind.

Styx's revenge only made it obvious how well he knew me.

He was silent for a long moment as he glared at the empty doorway. When he finally relaxed his guard, his laughter wheezed behind me, tickling the hair at the back of my neck. It wasn't human laughter by any means, but it was honest.

Revenge had never been sweeter.

Or stickier.

When Styx rose and began folding the blankets and placing them back on the shelves, I couldn't help but fall just a little harder for him.

The walk back home was chilly and awkward. My legs were wobbly and

I was hyper-aware of the way Styx's cum was leaking down the back of my thighs. He didn't lead the way this time. Instead, he followed behind me, making happy-growly noises whenever a fresh sluice of his pleasure slipped onto my skin.

Climbing the fence was the worst part, though it was worth it when I got halfway over and I got another thirty-seconds with Styx's tongue lapping at my sensitive hole.

Later, after we'd snuggled into bed, with Styx's feet hanging off the edge, I asked how he'd made sure Farmer Jones hadn't followed after us. He just smiled, Cheshire-like and just a little evil, pulled my knitted blanket over the both of us, and pressed a kiss to my forehead.

When Rotho jumped onto the bed, Styx didn't even complain.

And even though I was curious, I didn't ask again.

Chapter Eight

ON THE DAY of the Fall Festival I woke up refreshed and sore. Rotho yipped at me, annoyed that I'd slept in later than normal, despite the fact this had been an ongoing pattern for months. The sun had already risen, and I laughed, giddy, as memories from the night before flickered to the surface. I enjoyed them like a slideshow of debauchery, and I couldn't help but smile throughout my morning routine as I brewed my pot of tea and let Rotho out to do his business.

My mind was full of too-long tongues, slick uncut cocks, antlers, and yellow eyes.

I wouldn't win at the fair, not without a pumpkin, but it didn't matter so much anymore.

Not with the sore ache in my hips from a thorough fucking, and the promise of a repeat that night.

When I stepped out into the morning sunlight, I laughed, bright and surprised.

Because nestled at the back of my garden, just as they had been the morning before, were four large, orange pumpkins. They glistened in the light, covered in dew drops. Just looking at them, you would never know the carnage that had taken place the day before. I had to check my freezer for discarded pumpkin, to confirm that what I was seeing was real.

It was.

The freezer was full, and Styx had fixed what had been broken, just like he'd promised.

Getting into town with a massive pumpkin was harder than I'd anticipated. I managed somehow, with the help of nosy Marie. She chattered at me the entire drive over, her seat positioned as far forward as it could be so she could reach the pedals on her pickup truck.

Today, her dress was covered in jack-o-lanterns, barn cats, and candy corn.

When I smiled at her, she smiled back.

"You look different," she hummed thoughtfully, tapping her lip as we pulled into the overcrowded festival parking lot. "Did you get a haircut?"

I didn't know what to say, so I just nodded, even though it was a lie.

I felt different.

Freer.

Though anticipation still tangled around my heart.

Every year, the festival began with a breakfast buffet. The Mayor gave his speech, and the fire department and police department ate first. After they had packed their plates full and taken their seats, it was the City Council members' turn. Then came the business owners, and lastly, the general population.

I'd never participated in this part before, but today I did. Rotho sat patiently beside me while I waited in line, forced to chat with the people beside me out of necessity, as giddiness bubbled up inside me.

Somehow, deep down, I knew I would win today.

I would become Styx's Sacrifice as I was always meant to be.

"Have you seen Jones today?" Beth Anne from the general store asked me. I'd always liked Beth Anne. She was kinder than Tom, and though she laughed at Farmer Jones's inappropriate comments, I got the feeling she liked him about as much as I did. I'd asked her about it once, and she'd told me to leave it alone, that she had it covered.

I shook my head. "Not since yesterday."

"I heard he's got a nasty flu," she said, turning to her wife, who was cradling their two-year-old. She'd fallen asleep, too tired to handle the early start to the day, despite the fact it was already eight. Jane replied with a thoughtful hum, "His wife has it too—and all the farm hands. It's strange, don't you think? Every one of them getting sick, all at once."

I tried not to look too suspicious as I gathered several pancakes onto my plate, as well as a hearty helping of sausage.

"Probably one of those kids brought it onto the farm yesterday," Beth Anne concluded, turning back to me with a smile. "You best watch yourself, so you don't get sick, too. You're only a sneeze away from his whole horrible operation."

"I've got a great immune system," I said in reply, trying not to laugh as they both gave me a pitying look. My 'immune system' was named Styx, and apparently on top of growing magic pumpkins, and unlocking doors, he could also willfully make people sick.

I fed Rotho the sausage I'd grabbed while I picked at my pancakes, staring out at the crowd of people surrounding me. The town had grown in recent years, and I hadn't even noticed. It was far larger now than it had ever been when I was a child. I tried to feel the fear I always had when I was surrounded by a large group of people, but I couldn't.

I simply didn't care anymore.

Before I'd claimed I didn't care, but I always secretly had.

I'd thought I wanted them to like me. I'd wanted to fit in. It had taken me years to realize that what I'd actually wanted all along wasn't their approval. What I'd wanted was somewhere to belong.

Now I had that.

I had a family.

I had a best friend—who was currently begging for more sausage.

I had a lover.

I had someone to come home to.

I didn't need these people to like me. Now that I didn't care, it was a lot easier to talk to them. The pressure was gone. The town felt a fraction less scary, even if it was still unfamiliar and not the place I wanted to live in. I liked who I was. I'd always liked who I was. It was them, who had struggled, and they could continue to struggle. That wasn't my fault.

I didn't need to change to find where I belonged.

I'd just needed him.

Styx.

Sometimes home was a person, not a place, and that was okay.

Rotho's tongue lapped the sausage juice from my fingers and I laughed, turning away from the heavy gazes of the curious crowd. Maybe I imagined the way they looked at me. Because now, as I glanced around, no one was paying attention. Rotho placed a hairy paw on my knee and I snorted, amused.

"I'll get you more, bud," I promised, watching as he panted with the same happy smile he'd always had.

I got him more sausage.

And then it was time.

Destiny was calling.

Soon, it would all be over.

I won the pumpkin division.

I won, I won, *I won*.

Elation made my head spin as Marie Culberry pinned the blue ribbon to my chest, and offered me a secretive smile. The crowd was cheering—aside from the other produce competitors. They eyed me suspiciously, as if they thought I had cheated. Even the dark looks I received from the other participants weren't enough to calm the racing of my heart or the way my shoulders felt lighter than they ever had before.

"Congrats, dear," she murmured, close enough to me that no one else would be able to hear. "Between you and me, I'm glad that awful Farmer Jones came down with something. You would've won regardless with a beaut like that, but it's nice to see someone else win for once." She patted my hand, her eyes full of warmth. "June would be proud, you know." My heart wobbled. "Next time you make her famous pumpkin soup, promise you'll give me a call."

I promised, more than a little stunned as she made her way to the other participants to smooth down their ruffled feathers with a few well-placed compliments, and the hope for next year.

They were probably angry because without Jones here, all of them had gotten their hopes up.

My pumpkin sat atop a wooden palette, glistening in the afternoon light. It was brighter orange than the banners that decorated the festival and I couldn't help but glance toward the edge of the woods in anticipation.

Rotho's wet nose brushed the back of my hand, and I smiled brighter when I turned my attention back to Marie's retreating figure, catching her right before she slipped outside the tent.

June would be proud of you, you know.

"Thank you!" I called quietly, and Marie swiveled, flashing me a pleased little smile and a finger wave. Then she was gone, off to judge the next division. There were three rounds of produce judging before I'd know whether or not I'd won best overall.

I could feel the end in sight.

Sacrifice.

I had no idea what lay in store for me at the end of this path, but I was aching with the desire to find out.

I didn't want to waste the day agonizing over the other divisions, so I took my blue ribbon and my dog, and headed to the food trucks. Rotho and I gorged ourselves on as many food items as we could. With each dollar I spent, I felt lighter and lighter, my fingers coated in powdered sugar as I snarfed down a funnel cake and watched Rotho pick apart a hot dog to eat only the meat.

A few hours passed, and I enjoyed myself, wandering through the crowd. People of all shapes, sizes, and ages chatted and laughed–sharing treats and stories, as they participated in the game booths that lined the walkway. At the end of the row sat the platform the Sacrifice would end up on, and behind it, always present, was the shadow of the woods.

The sun disappeared behind the horizon as the Ferris wheel burst to life. I watched it spin for a long time, listening to the laughter that bounced between stars as I waited for the loudspeakers to announce who had won.

"And… the winner for best produce this year goes to…" My heart was in my throat as I strained to hear the speaker closest to me, willing the world to be quiet–for once–so I could listen.

Over the sound of chatter and laughter, a name rang out like a promise in the night sky.

My name.

"Ellis Clearwater!"

The ceremony took longer than I'd anticipated. Rotho side-eyed me the entire time as I was painted head to toe in red. The attendants took my clothes and dressed me in a pair of spandex shorts as they had always done to Sacrifices of the past. I'd watched this same ritual from the outside countless times as a child and a young adult, before Aunt June and Uncle Ruth had died and I'd stopped going.

After the paint came the ribbons. Blue ribbons laced up my limbs, decorating my body in a semblance of modesty. I felt like a pig, trussed up for the slaughter, and I realized belatedly that centuries ago—when the tradition had first begun—that's exactly what being a Sacrifice had meant.

What was going to happen tonight?

Would something change?

There were hundreds of Sacrifices between me and the last disappearance. All this time… *all this time,* maybe I'd been making up the significance of this in my head. Maybe nothing was going to happen tonight. Maybe I'd wake in the morning with dew for a crown, a crick in my back from being tied to the pedestal, the same man I'd woken up as this morning.

Maybe.

Or maybe… maybe, no matter what happened now… I would still be changed forever. Because Styx had changed me—with every laugh, with every shared meal; his companionship and courtship—maybe *that* was something I'd carry all the way to the grave, until I had soil for my palace and nothing but peace for company.

Looping round my arms and legs, they tied me to the platform with ribbons that connected to the anchors at the bottom of the stage. The entire festival could see me up here, and I watched as pale heads tipped toward me, curious, just as I had been as a child. I had never, in all my life, thought I would do this.

But then again, I'd also never anticipated falling in love with Styx.

A cute little girl with pigtails pointed up at me and her mother smiled, leaning down to whisper in her ear. Maybe she was telling her the story of the Sacrifice, as June had told me when I was that age.

Stars flickered behind my eyelids even when I shut them—like magic.

Rotho panted beside me, his head flopped over his front legs, his tail thumping against the stage. *Thump, thump. Thump, thump.* My heart matched its steady pace. When I asked for a bowl of water for him, the women who had prepped me cooed and flirted. "You're so attentive," they praised, and I just laughed, because it didn't mean anything. Flirting with humans still felt as off as it had before I'd met my beast.

Now I understood why, all this time, I could never form real connections. After all, none of them were my mate.

For hours, I waited.

The moon climbed high in the sky.

Stars danced.

The whisper of wind caressed my cheek like a friend, pushing my bangs out of my face as red paint dried sticky and suffocating along my bare skin.

Cicadas chirped.

The Ferris wheel emptied.

The crowd dispersed, one family at a time, figures bobbing in a colorful parade to the entrance as the shops and food carts all flickered into darkness. The lights shut off. Then it was just me, the sky, Rotho, and my anticipation.

I waited.

I waited.

I waited.

I waited.

I waited.

The indigo sky was turning lavender and a sinking feeling settled like a pit in my stomach as I dropped my head low, and felt the weight of the world begin to settle once again. Soon, I would no longer be weightless. I would no longer be free.

He wasn't coming.

Once again, my imagination had gotten the best of me.

Just as I'd given up hope, Rotho rose from his spot at my feet to point at the forest, his tail wagging in greeting. He tipped his head back and howled. The hair along the back of my arms rose and I straightened, tipping my face toward the woods, desperation running through my veins in place of blood. My hands were sweaty, my heart skittered wildly against my ribcage.

Elation, fear, and relief flooded through me.

A broad-shouldered, familiar shadowy figure approached, his willowy frame blending in with the trees behind him as he stepped gracefully outside of the forest. His long legs slipped between the blades of grass, but there was no sound aside from the whisper of the wind. Naked and gorgeous, his thighs flexed and his soft cock shifted from side to side with every careful step he took. His ebony claws glinted when they caught the light, a gorgeous smattering of dark hair trailing from his belly button down to his frankly massive dick.

I couldn't look away.

My name is Styx, the wind murmured.

You have entered my forest.

You have accepted my gifts.

From the moment I saw you, I knew you were mine.

He could see me on my pedestal.

Just like always, he didn't turn away.

One foot at a time, he closed the distance between us. His eyes were warm, his lips pulled into a serious, lovestruck smile. I had never, in all my life, thought someone could look at me like that. And when his smile morphed into a grin, I knew it was because he saw the same exact expression mirrored on my face.

We were a pair of lovestruck fools.

My breath caught as he continued to close the distance between us. Stuttering, stuttering, stuttering—my heart threatened to escape my chest as adrenaline coursed through my blood. *Run to him.* That's what my body was telling me: *run to him to escape the shackles of human life.*

Tied to the platform, I had no choice but to ignore my instincts.

It was human nature to avoid the things you didn't understand. I suppose I'd always made a pretty odd human.

Maybe I stayed because I was in love, maybe I was simply stupid.

Or maybe, *just maybe*, deep down Styx sensed what I did. That we were two ships at sea, our paths crossing in an anomaly that would rewrite our course for the rest of time.

His antlers climbed toward the lilac colored clouds, shrouded in a shadow from the rising sun behind him, as his overgrown curls obscured the vast majority of what I knew to be a devastatingly handsome face. I'd never been so enraptured by someone before, so stunned, so…floored.

Step by step, he prowled across the fairgrounds to claim me, the hoot of owls in the trees, and the chirp of crickets blanketing his approach.

He was silence. He was strength. He was the earth itself.

And now, he was *mine*.

There are two monsters in the woods.
That's what the stories like to say.
With gnashing teeth,
And wind for wings,
Little children are their prey.

There are two monsters in the woods.
One stole the other in light of day.
He found a mate,
To hunt beside him,
So you must never stray.

There are two monsters in the woods.
The lonely monster cries no more,
You'll hear them sing,
A song of fate,
Their happiness impossible to ignore.

Author Note

THANK YOU SO much to everyone who finished *There's a Monster in the Woods*! I hope you enjoyed your adventure with Styx and Ellis (Stellis), and I can't wait to see you for my next spooky release.

Special thanks to all those who made the creation of this book possible, especially Molly with her creative artsy genius, Jess, the world's best cheerleader, Kat, who dedicated hours to reading and rereading the book for me, despite having a release of their own (Go check out anything by K.L. Hiers for more paranormal MM fun!) and the lovely, wonderful Bermi who let me screech at them as I wrote. I am also incredibly grateful to my wonderful hubby Mr. Quin, for loving me even when the excessive caffeine I consumed while writing made me crash and burn. His love and support always keeps me going, and his endless patience has allowed me to grow and change because he catches me every time I fall.

Thank you to everyone who contributed their time, energy, and love to this project; you are all my dear friends. And most of all, thank you to the reader, because without you, the creation of this story would have been meaningless. I write the words, but you are the ones who bring the story to life. Each and every one of you is priceless. Thank you for falling in love with these characters alongside me. I love all of you so much. See you next time!

Love, **FAE**

About Fae

FAE IS OBSESSED with anything romance. From a young age she realized she had a passion for falling in love over and over again. She loves to tell stories through both her art and writing. With a passion for classical monsters, meet-cutes, and contemporary romance, you can often find her with her nose stuck in a book and her pet corgi, Champa, on her lap.

She currently resides in Utah with her amazing husband and her collection of squishmallows. When you read one of her books, you can expect to find love stories between humans, monsters, and loveable assholes that will make you laugh (and cry) as you get lost in their worlds for just a little while. Every story comes with a happily ever after guarantee.

Find her online at:
WWW.FAELOVESART.COM